LIVI

Frank and the Chamber of Fear

Illustrated by Derek Brazell

PUFFIN BOOKS

PUFFIN BOOKS

Published by the Penguin Group
Penguin Books Ltd, 80 Strand, London WC2R 0RL, England
Penguin Putnam Inc., 375 Hudson Street, New York, New York 10014, USA
Penguin Books Australia Ltd, 250 Camberwell Road, Camberwell, Victoria 3124, Australia
Penguin Books Canada Ltd, 10 Alcorn Avenue, Toronto, Ontario, Canada M4V 3B2
Penguin Books India (P) Ltd, 11 Community Centre, Panchsheel Park,
New Delhi – 110 017, India
Penguin Books (NZ) Ltd, Cnr Rosedale and Airborne Roads, Albany, Auckland, New Zealand
Penguin Books (South Africa) (Pty) Ltd, 24 Sturdee Avenue, Rosebank 2196, South Africa

Penguin Books Ltd, Registered Offices: 80 Strand, London WC2R 0RL, England

www.penguin.com

First published 2003
1

Set in 13/18pt Bembo

Made and printed in England by Clays Ltd, St Ives plc

British Library Cataloguing in Publication Data
A CIP catalogue record for this book is available from the British Library

ISBN 0-141-31429-X

Contents

FRANK'S HOUSE
Guy lives here
MABEL'S HOUSE
Tania and her Mum and Dad live here
BRIGHT ST.
13
11
9

The Hamsters of Bright Street
GEORGE'S HOUSE
Jackie, Jake and Josh live here
ELSIE'S HOUSE
Lucy, Tom and their Mum and Dad live here
7
5
3
1
The WILD

This book is dedicated to Yvonne, of Bright Street, hamster-friend extraordinaire.

And especial thanks to Ian Hunton and Roy Darbyhire for their helpful advice, and to the Friends of Frank, including Paul and Ben, Joe Coop, Gus, Grace and Charlie Johnston, Georgina Lambert, Patrick Joseph and Griff Simmons-Roberts, and Gregg Taylor.

Livi Michael has two sons, Paul and Ben, a dog called Jenny and a hamster called Frank. She has written books for adults before, but ever since getting to know Frank has had the sense that he had a story that should be told. So here it is, and both Livi and Frank hope you enjoy it very much.

Foreword

This is a story about a hamster called Frank, who lives at number 13 Bright Street. Bright Street is a short, sloping row of terraced houses, and three other hamsters live there. Mabel, a plump white hamster, lives at number 11, and two of her cubs, Elsie and George, live at numbers 3 and 5 respectively.

Frank has met all these other hamsters on the many occasions when he has escaped from his cage, and from his owner, Guy. Frank is always getting out. He likes to explore. Although Guy had bought Frank from Mr Wiggs' pet shop, which was only two streets away, Frank, like others of his kind, actually came from the vast deserts of Syria. Frank doesn't know where Syria is, but he knows that he doesn't belong in a cage, in a little house on Bright Street.

The other hamsters aren't as adventurous as Frank. They are afraid of getting lost; of being eaten in the Wild, or, worst of all, of being preyed upon by a mysterious creature they know only as the Black Hamster of Narkiz. Of them all, only Frank has actually met the Black Hamster of Narkiz. But instead of leading him to his doom, he had taken Frank into the Wild, and shown him the power and the glory of the tribe of Hamster. Since that time, many weeks had passed, and Frank is still waiting and hoping to see the Black Hamster again.

The other thing you need to know about Frank is that he has a motto, and that motto is 'Courage'. When he says it to himself it always has an exclamation mark after it like this: 'Courage!'

1 Danger!

All was quiet on Bright Street. The pub had closed and the last stragglers had made their way home, singing. In the seven houses that faced the waste ground, the lights had gone off one by one – first in the children's bedrooms, then downstairs, then upstairs in the adults' bedrooms.

The last person to go to bed was Mrs Wheeler, who lived in Mabel's house. She had taken to crocheting lace last thing at night while the house was quiet and she could watch some late-night telly. But soon even her eyes were drooping and she yawned and stretched and turned off the TV.

'Night-night, Mabel,' she said to the rather splendid-looking white hamster who had just got up. She paused and watched Mabel as she filled her pouches with food.

'You're a funny little thing,' Mrs Wheeler said, tapping on the cage. 'What do you do all night, eh?'

'Mind your own business,' Mabel thought, staring back at her beadily. Mrs Wheeler gave a little laugh.

'Listen to me, talking to a hamster,' she said. 'Just as

if you could understand.' And she turned off the light and went upstairs.

'Just as if I could understand indeed,' Mabel thought snappily as she climbed into her little buggy for some exercise. 'You can talk, lady. I've had better conversations with my bedding.'

Mabel stared around for a moment in satisfaction. Hamsters' eyes work better in the dark. Mabel could work out the different shapes more clearly and get a better sense of the room. She loved the feeling of having the place to herself, of being queen in her own domain.

'At last,' she thought, as the toilet flushed upstairs, then the bathroom door opened and the bedroom door clicked shut. 'A nice, quiet, peaceful night.'

But she couldn't have been more wrong.

Some time later there was a muffled thudding from the kitchen, and the sound of glass tinkling on to the floor. There was the click of a lock and the sound of someone moving about as though trying not to be heard.

Mabel's nostrils filled with the smell of strange human. She stiffened and bristled all over. A ray of light moved under the kitchen door, then, as the door opened, it flared into a beam that travelled all over the front room.

'Ow!' Mabel squeaked as it shone right into her eyes. She wanted to run, but stayed, transfixed by the glare.

'There you are,' a strange voice breathed. 'And aren't you a beauty?'

Mabel began to retreat, but she was listening. It was a hoarse, gravelly voice, and it murmured at her admiringly in a soothing way.

'Just look at that coat,' it said. 'What a bobby-dazzler. Are you white all over?'

As he said this the man propped his torch up by the cage and began pulling apart the tubes that connected one part of Mabel's cage to another.

'Hey, watch it!' Mabel said, and she ran to the back of her cage.

'Now, don't be shy,' said the voice. 'Go on, give us a twirl.'

Mabel had a brief impression of a large, oval face, bluish and stubbly at the bottom end, but with very little hair on top, which was where hair should be, according to Mabel's experience of humans. The man smelled of leather and cigarettes, and there were such large pouches beneath his eyes that Mabel thought that must be where he kept his food. He leaned closer, breathing all over Mabel, which was not pleasant.

'Let's have a proper look at you,' he said.

Mabel's ears flattened and she bared her teeth.

'Now, don't be like that,' the voice said. 'You're a real find, you are – look at that thick, silky fur. You're wasted in a place like this. How'd you like to come with Uncle Vince? I'd treat you like royalty.'

Mabel hesitated. 'Royalty?' she thought. But as the man spoke he pressed a plastic plug into the place where her connecting tube should have been, and Mabel was sealed into a single room.

'All right, my beauty,' he said. 'Off we go.'

'What?' squeaked Mabel. 'What do you mean? Put me down at once!'

For the man had lifted the sealed unit containing Mabel and was carrying her out of the room!

'How dare you!' Mabel squeaked as she felt a blast of cold air from the back door. 'You won't get away with this. Put me down at once – do you hear?'

But there was no reply.

Elsie had been having a confusing time. She hadn't slept all day because she was so used to sleeping in Lucy's room. But now Lucy's bedroom was being decorated, and Elsie had been moved into the lounge – much to the delight of Lucy's brother, Thomas, who now had a chance to play with her. But Elsie was disturbed by this new arrangement. She had stayed in her bedroom at first, without sleeping, and had then moved her bedding twice. She hadn't eaten at all, and had scurried behind her wheel when Thomas tried to play with her.

'She won't let me take her out,' he complained.

'That's because she's *my* hamster,' Lucy said, rather smugly. But in fact Elsie didn't want to play even with Lucy.

'Leave her alone,' Lucy's mother said. 'She'll get used to it.'

But Elsie hadn't got used to it. She had been downstairs before on her own, exploring, but only when the house was dark and quiet. Now there were hundreds of different smells from this room and the kitchen, and a lot more noise from the TV. So much noise, in fact, that she couldn't get a proper sense of the room. Hamsters don't have very good eyesight and rely a lot more on hearing and smell to understand their surroundings. Only now, when everyone had gone to bed, did Elsie feel that it was safe to come out for a good sniff around. But first she worked off some of her nervous energy by running round her wheel.

'Now,' she thought, when she had finished her exercise, 'time for a good look around.'

But just as she was thinking this, the door between the front room and the kitchen opened, and a bright 'O' of light shone on the wall facing Elsie's cage.

Elsie stared, fascinated, as it dipped and rose over one surface then another – the curtains, the bureau, the television. She had no idea what it was, it was something totally outside her experience, but then, so had everything else been that day. She wasn't even alarmed until it reached her. Then she flattened herself to the floor of her cage, with her ears pressed back against her skull.

'Hello,' said a deep, rasping voice. 'You're a nice little thing. A bit dark, but still – nice pelt.'

Even in her state of nervous alarm Elsie thought that this was quite a personal thing to say as an introduction. She glared at the man as he peered in at her cage. Was he the decorator? Lucy's dad had said a lot of bad things about the decorator because he hadn't turned up, and Lucy's dad had started the job himself. If this was the decorator now, he really was late. Did he look like a decorator? Elsie didn't know. He had a baggy, saggy kind of a face with pouches under his eyes and a big pouch under his chin.

'You could keep a lot of food in there,' Elsie thought.

The next minute, she shot backwards as he lifted the lid off her cage and inserted thick yellowish fingers inside it.

'Come and play with Uncle Vince,' he said.

The fingers smelled strongly of tobacco. Elsie bared her teeth and prepared to bite them. It was time for all the tactics she had once taught George – the Threatening Stance and the War Cry and the Drawing of Blood. Elsie took a deep breath and prepared to rear into her most frightening pose, but then the man replaced the lid.

'Suit yourself,' he said.

Then, just as he had with Mabel's cage, he began

disconnecting the tubes and plugging the openings so that Elsie was sealed into a single unit. She ran around it in alarm.

'What are you doing?' she squeaked. 'Stop it at once!'

But Uncle Vince didn't appear to be listening. Elsie slid from one side of her chamber to the other as he picked her up.

'Where are you taking me?' she squeaked as he opened the kitchen door.

'Lucy!' she squeaked as loudly as she could. '*Lucy!*'

But Lucy was fast asleep upstairs.

2 Caught

Out into the cold night air Elsie went, bumping and slithering about until she gave up the attempt to see where they were going and curled herself into a pile of wood-shavings, and hid.

'It's a bad dream,' she told herself, trembling all over. 'When I open my eyes again I'll be back in Lucy's room.'

But of course she wasn't. When she finally heard a door open and felt the air change, she stayed where she was for several moments, afraid to look. She felt Vince set her down on a wooden surface. There was a strong smell of hamster in the room – of more than one hamster in fact – and an equally strong smell of food. And among all the confusing smells there were one or two that were very familiar.

Cautiously Elsie stuck the quivering tip of her nose out of the wood-shavings, but whisked it back again smartly as Vince lifted the lid from her cage.

'There you are, old girl,' he said. 'Have a treat on me.'

'Old girl indeed,' Elsie thought. But the food did smell delicious, especially since Elsie had gone so long without eating. When nothing else happened, Elsie warily peeped out. She could hear other hamsters scuffling and murmuring.

'I wonder who it is?'

'Let's have a look, then.'

'She doesn't want to come out.'

Then there was a sniffing sound and a voice so familiar that if she hadn't been crouched down she might well have fallen over.

'I know who it is,' the voice said. 'It's Elsie!'

Astonished, Elsie pushed first her nose then the rest of her head out of her hiding place, and stared around in wonder at the blurred images of the room.

'George,' she said, 'is it really you?' And the blurred images resolved themselves into a single image of a hamster so like Elsie they might have been twins (as in fact they were), beaming at her from behind the bars of his cage.

'Elsie!' he said.

Elsie ran to the see-through wall of her own cage.

'Oh George!' she said.

'Oh dear,' said Mabel's voice. 'Just when I was beginning to enjoy myself.'

Elsie turned in astonishment.

'Mabel?' she said. 'What are you doing here?'

'Mother to you,' Mabel said, through a mouthful of food. 'Or madam.'

But Elsie wasn't listening. She was staring around the room at what seemed like dozens of hamster faces, all staring back.

'What are you doing here?' she said. 'What are any of us doing here?'

There was a moment's silence, then Mabel said, 'Well, personally, I'm having a good time.' And all the other hamsters agreed with her.

'Best food we've had in ages.'

'Lovely and warm.'

'And a nice cage all to myself!' said a whitish hamster with grey patches, next to George.

'It's better now you're here, though,' George said, beaming at her as though he would never stop. 'This is Daisy, by the way,' he added, waving at the grey and white hamster. 'Daisy, this is my sister Elsie.'

Daisy was swinging from the bars of her cage.

'Hmm, well, I suppose she does look like you,' she said. 'Only she's nowhere near as good-looking.'

George laughed in an embarrassed kind of way. 'Heh heh heh,' he said.

'And she looks a lot older,' Daisy added, dangling upside-down now.

Elsie thought this was very rude.

'Mind your manners,' she said.

Daisy glanced at her briefly.

'Can you do this?' she said, and she did a perfect somersault from the bars of her cage on to her bed.

'Why would I want to?' said Elsie, witheringly.

'Hoity-toity,' Daisy said. 'Is she your mum, then,' she added, nodding at Mabel. 'You don't look anything like her.'

'Of course not,' Mabel said, her mouth full. 'They're both runts. *I'm* a pure albino.'

'I wouldn't want to look like her,' Elsie said. 'Now, do you mind if I talk to my brother?'

Daisy scampered across her cage until she was quite close to George.

'Is she always this snooty?' she asked in a loud whisper.

George looked uncomfortable. Elsie drew in her breath sharply and there might soon have been a quarrel, but another voice chipped in.

'Here, George,' it said, 'aren't you going to introduce the rest of us?'

'Oh, of course,' George said hastily. 'Elsie – this is Chestnut.'

Elsie's eyes focused with difficulty on Chestnut, who was further away on a bureau against the wall. He was a rather elderly hamster, round and sandy-brown, with a cheery, smiling face. Elsie wasn't used to being introduced to other hamsters. She'd lived on her own in a cage since being a young cub, but she knew how to behave.

'Charmed, I'm sure,' she said with dignity.

'She doesn't talk like you either,' Daisy said in the same loud whisper.

'And this is Maurice,' George said quickly, turning to a sleek and glossy hamster with a lot of yellow teeth, who was in a cage on a coffee table.

'Dazzled,' said Maurice, with a deep bow.

'And this,' said George, turning round, 'is Felicity, and her son, Drew.'

Elsie turned round as well. As her eyes adjusted she could see that there was rather a lot of furniture in the room, a great assortment of chairs and tables. Felicity's cage was on a set of bookshelves propped up against the wall. There were a lot of other empty cages on the shelves too.

Felicity was a pale golden hamster with a practical, maternal air. She was busy grooming Drew, a small, grey cub with sticky fur, and only paused briefly to say, 'Pleased to meet you,' before holding Drew firmly and licking his ears.

Elsie stared around the room. Once again she had the sensation that she must be dreaming. The room was lit by a low red light and was very warm. There was a pleasant, drowsy smell which made it hard to think clearly. But she felt that she must think clearly. Where had all these hamsters come from, and why were there so many cages? Elsie shook her head, as if to rearrange her thoughts.

'But – where have you come from?' she said. 'How did you get here?'

'From Mr Wiggs' pet shop, of course,' Daisy said. 'Somebody's bought us at last.'

'I thought it'd never happen,' Chestnut said with a sigh.

Elsie opened her mouth to say that she hadn't come from the pet shop, but another thought occurred to her.

'What about all these cages?' she said. 'Were there other hamsters here?'

For the first time Chestnut looked uncomfortable.

'There were other hamsters when I got here,' he said. 'But they've all gone now. I don't know why – maybe Uncle Vince bought them as presents for his friends.'

'Who cares,' said Mabel, still chomping. 'More food for us.'

Maurice smiled his yellow smile. 'Isn't she magnificent,' he said.

Elsie shook her head again. 'Uncle who?'

'Uncle Vince, of course,' said Daisy. 'Same as brought you here.'

'And provided all this delicious food,' said Mabel.

Elsie looked at the food. It certainly was good. There were baby corn cobs and some grated carrot, cashew nuts and apple, even a chunk of pepperami sausage.

'Go on, tuck in,' said Chestnut. 'It's a big improvement on the pet shop.'

Elsie knew there was something she should say, but it was hard to remember.

She fought hard to clear her brain.

'But I'm not from the pet shop,' she said slowly. 'Neither are you,' she said to George. 'Or you,' she added, turning to Mabel. Elsie stared at them. 'We've all got Owners,' she said. 'What about our Owners?'

'We've got a better Owner now,' said Mabel, and for once it looked as though George agreed with her.

'It's much nicer here, Els,' he said. 'Especially now you're here. Nobody torments you. Uncle Vince always remembers our food.'

'We've all got our own cages,' Chestnut put in.

'Drew can stay with me,' Felicity said. 'I was always so worried that he'd be taken away.'

'And it's always nice and warm,' said Daisy. 'Hurray!'

Elsie didn't know what to think or say. She had always had her own cage, of course, in a nice warm room, and was always fed. She was very fond of her Owner. Next to George, Lucy was the person who mattered most in the world.

But somehow, in this warm room with the heavy scent, and the strange experience of meeting new hamsters, it was hard to remember any of this. She stared in bewilderment at her food.

'It's a lot to take in at first,' Chestnut said kindly. 'I was very put out at first – couldn't make sense of it at all. I've lived in a pet shop all my life, and I'm no cub. But it's very pleasant here – you couldn't wish for a nicer place. And Uncle Vince – well – he treats us like royalty.'

'Of course he does,' said Mabel, and Maurice smiled again.

'You are royalty, my princess,' he said.

Elsie looked at George, who smiled at her encouragingly.

'It is a bit strange at first,' he said. 'But Elsie – we're together!'

Elsie couldn't help smiling back. She picked up a

creamy yellow cashew nut and held it in both paws. It certainly smelled good. She bit a chunk off it. It tasted good. Quickly she pushed all the nuts into her pouch at once to eat later in her bed. She felt a bit shy about eating in front of strange hamsters. Then she started on the sweetcorn and carrot, making room in her pouches by rubbing them. She had forgotten how hungry she was. It was a bigger bowl of food than she was used to. There was hardly room for it all in her pouches. She had to eat some and pack the rest in tightly. When she had finished she felt extraordinarily tired.

'I must have a little sleep,' she muttered. Things would seem clearer to her when she woke up. And after all, she told herself, if George said it was all right, it probably was. She looked around for the best place to make her bed.

And then a thought came to her: 'She, Mabel and George were here, but what about Frank? If Frank was here, he would know what to do.' Elsie stood on her hind legs and looked all around the room, whiskers twitching.

'Isn't Frank here?' she said to George. 'Where's Frank?'

3 Frank Comes Home

'There you are, Frank,' said Guy, putting Frank's cage back on its usual ledge. 'It's good to have you back.'

'At last!' Frank thought, and he ran from one corner of his cage to another, sniffing the familiar smells of Guy's front room.

Guy had been away at a music festival, and he had left Frank with his sister Mary, her son Luke, and Luke's dog, Rex.

Fortunately it had only been for the weekend, but Frank had had quite enough. Luke had been delighted to have a hamster again. He always liked having Frank to stay, though he hadn't been too keen on looking after his own hamster. A weekend was just long enough for Luke to stay excited about hamster care, and he had brought all his friends round to play with Frank. They had made him run up and down the sleeves of their jumpers, then across a mini-football pitch while they fired balls at him, and then they put him inside Luke's remote-control car and whizzed him around the room until Luke's friend Tariq said that Frank had probably had enough. Much to his relief, they put him back in his cage.

'Now I know what George went through,' he thought.

George lived at number 5 Bright Street with two little boys called Jake and Josh. They didn't mean to be rough, but they were always, well, *experimenting*. And their idea of fun was to see if George could run round the wheel of a washing-machine or operate a robot from the inside. George had also had problems with their big white cat, Sergeant. Now Frank was experiencing for the first time what it was like to live with a dog.

As soon as Rex saw Frank, he ran at the cage, barking furiously. Deafened, Frank ran behind his wheel.

'Courage!' he told himself, and he flattened himself to the floor and shut his eyes.

Mary pulled Rex away.

'Luke, you're going to have to be careful about Rex,' she said. 'You know this kind of dog's trained to hunt rodents.'

'Oh wonderful,' Frank thought. 'What was Guy doing, leaving him in this death trap?'

Even when Rex was out of the room, the smell of dog was overpowering to Frank and he couldn't settle. And whenever Rex was in the room he ran straight to Frank's cage and stood with his big wet nose pressed up against the bars, blasting Frank with his doggy breath and wagging his tail so eagerly that it caused a great draught and all Frank's wood-shavings blew about.

And he was, if possible, even less intelligent than Guy.

'Go – away,' Frank told him firmly, but there was no sign of response in the enormous doggy eyes. He just went on gazing at Frank as if there was nothing else in the world to look at, and then, to add to the horror, a great strand of dog-slobber spooled its way through the bars of the cage towards Frank. Frank leapt to one side just in time, but a big drop splashed right into his food bowl. He was absolutely disgusted.

'That's it,' he told himself. 'I'm not staying here to be dribbled on. The first chance I get, I'm off.'

He spent most of the first day curled up tightly in his bed and, unusually, he slept through the night. But the next day Luke took him out for exercise in his hamster globe.

By now Frank was expert at getting out of his globe. He had chewed the plastic lid so much that it didn't fit properly. Guy normally stuck it down with Sellotape, but Frank thought Luke might forget. And he was right. As soon as Luke put him down, Frank pushed against the lid. It opened a chink and at once he began to squeeze his way out.

Just at that moment the doorbell rang, and Luke, not noticing that Frank was getting out, ran to answer it. Soon Frank's head and front paws were out of the globe, but his back legs and tail were still in it. He was just looking for a way out of the room when Rex bounded in through the open door and charged at Frank in a snarling rush.

Fortunately, Frank's motto was 'Courage!' He kicked backwards and the globe smacked Rex smartly on the nose. This confused him just long enough for Frank to wriggle fully out of the globe and scuttle beneath a chair. There he stayed while Luke dragged Rex back into the kitchen. Frank hoped to make his way from there to the skirting-board, though he had no clear idea of where he would go from there, but then Tariq spotted him.

'There he is,' he said, and he moved the chair carefully so that he wouldn't hurt Frank.

Frank moved with it. He had no intention of coming out, not even when they offered him crisps. Finally Tariq lifted the chair and Luke scooped Frank up carefully and returned him to his cage. They kept a close eye on him for the rest of the day, and they put Rex in the garden, so in the end Frank did begin to feel more settled. Then all Luke's friends came over to play with him, and by night-time he was so exhausted that he surprised himself by sleeping again instead of making a bid to escape.

The next morning Guy came back. The main band hadn't turned up, he said, and it had rained so much that everything was sinking slowly into the mud, including the bands. Someone had offered him a lift home and he had come straight away to see Frank.

'How is he?' Guy said, and his face lit up when he saw Frank peering at him through the bars. 'I bet you've had a fine old time.'

For once Frank was very pleased to see Guy – so pleased that he forgot to be cross. He was even prepared to put up with the cheese and chutney sandwiches, the singing and guitar-playing and the loud TV. But, of course, he couldn't let Guy off the hook altogether . . .

You should know that after Frank's encounter with the mysterious being known to hamsters as the Black Hamster of Narkiz (Narkiz is the name they give to their ancient territory beneath the sands of Syria), he had discovered that he had a strange kind of power over Guy. If Guy was relaxed and not thinking about anything in particular (which was most of the time), Frank could think his thoughts into Guy's head and make Guy do what he wanted.

This was a very useful skill, as you can imagine, and had improved Frank's quality of life no end. He now got proper hamster food instead of cheese and chutney sandwiches. He could make Guy turn off the TV from time to time and take Frank out of his cage for exercise. He even got Guy to carry Frank about with him in his shirt pocket when he went into other rooms, and once when he went to the shops. But Frank's skill didn't always work.

For one thing, Guy had to be there, where Frank could see him. Frank had found that out on his first day at Luke's, when he had tried hard to contact Guy and make him come back right away. Also, if Guy was really concentrating on what he was doing, then Frank couldn't seem to reach him. He'd had to work really hard to stop Guy from plastering over the gap beneath the gas fire, which was Frank's access to the Spaces Between and to the different houses on Bright Street. Frank managed to distract Guy once, but the second time Guy was determined, and he only stopped when the gas man came to read the meter.

And now Frank had discovered that this skill didn't seem to work on other humans – and definitely not on dogs, which was a bit discouraging. In fact Frank wasn't sure how much use it was as a gift, though it did help to entertain him in the evenings. Sometimes he would make Guy watch telly standing on his head, or eat a large bowl of hamster food as a punishment for feeding Frank on cheese and chutney sandwiches.

But what Frank really wanted to know was, what was it for? Was he supposed to use this strange skill to try to get back to his ancestral home, and to take other hamsters with him? And if so, how? The other hamsters he'd met so far didn't seem very keen on following him into the Wild, let alone Syria. In fact, the only person who really seemed to want to be with him was Guy.

Frank just wished the Black Hamster would return and tell him what to do. He had tried sending out thought-messages to him, and willing him to appear, but nothing happened. Sometimes this made Frank feel cheated and cross. Then he would make Guy do things for fun, like stand in the corner of the room with a lampshade on his head, or bark madly at the door when someone knocked.

But now Frank was pleased to be back, and Guy was pleased to see him, so he allowed Guy to pick up his guitar and sing a song to him:

'F and r, F and r
What do those two letters stand for?
Well, they stand for Frank and they stand for friend,
They stand for a friendship that'll never end.'

As Guy's songs went, it wasn't one of the worst, though he did sing it a few times too often. He told Frank all about the festival, and how he'd jammed on stage with a few other guitarists. Then he went to make his cheese and chutney sandwiches before settling down for the evening in front of the TV.

This took him quite some time, since Frank kept making him take them upstairs and flush them down the toilet one by one. Guy carried on chatting cheerfully to Frank while he did this and eventually Frank relented, and let him keep just one. And Guy was just about to switch on the TV and sit down to eat this sandwich when there was a knock at the front door.

For once Frank didn't make Guy run at the door and jump up at it, barking. Guy was cross enough already about having his snack interrupted. He took a great bite of it and tugged the door open. There, to his and Frank's surprise, stood Jackie.

'Hi,' she said. 'I hope you don't mind me calling by like this – but, well – you've got a hamster, haven't you?'

Guy could only look surprised, and nod with his mouth full.

'Is he all right?' Jackie went on. 'Only the police might want to talk to you.'

Guy looked even more surprised.

'The police?' he managed to say at last. 'Why? You don't need a licence for them, do you?'

'Haven't you heard?' Jackie said, and she held up a copy of the local paper.

LOCK UP YOUR HAMSTERS

it said, and there was a photograph of Mr Wiggs looking worried.

'You don't know, do you?' said Jackie as Guy stared. 'All the hamsters have been stolen!'

'No way!' said Guy. 'What's going on?'

4 Frank to the Rescue

Frank ran to the front of his cage and clutched the bars. *All* the hamsters stolen! This was terrible! What could it mean?

'That's terrible!' said Guy. 'You'd better come in.'

Jackie walked past Guy and spotted Frank.

'Is this your hamster?' she said, squatting in front of Frank's cage. 'He's lovely.'

'Never mind about that,' Frank thought. 'Tell me what's happened.'

'What's happened?' said Guy.

Jackie's eyes filled with tears and she blew her nose loudly.

'I miss George,' she said.

Then she stood up and told Guy the story of that awful night. While Frank had been away, someone had broken into numbers 3, 5 and 11 Bright Street and taken the hamsters away. Windows had been smashed and locks forced, but nothing else had been touched. Only the hamsters had gone.

'The kids are really upset,' Jackie said. 'It's not very nice, is it – someone breaking into your house? Jake and Josh don't want to sleep on their own any more, in case the thief comes back. And it's not just here – the pet shop's been broken into as well. And other hamsters have been disappearing in the last few weeks, the paper says. But it's odd that whoever it was knew just which houses to break into.' She looked at Guy. 'It's strange that your hamster's still here.'

'He's been away,' Guy said. 'At my sister's house – I've been to a festival.' He looked at Jackie. 'I've got witnesses.'

'Oh,' said Jackie. 'Well, I expect the police'll still want to talk to you.'

Guy didn't look too happy about this and Frank could see why. But the idea of anyone suspecting Guy was ridiculous. It would only hold things up until they caught the real villain. Frank could see that he would have to do that himself.

Jackie and Guy went on talking, about festivals and groups, and Guy's guitar-playing, while Frank ran around his cage in a fever of impatience. George, Elsie and Mabel missing – and he didn't know about it! Poor Elsie – poor George! They didn't like being out of their own territory at the best of times. Frank had to do something, but he didn't know what. And he couldn't do anything while Jackie and Guy were still there. He tried concentrating on Guy to make him send Jackie away, but he couldn't get through at all. Guy was looking at Jackie in much the same way as Luke's dog had looked at Frank. And Jackie seemed really interested in Guy's guitar.

'Go on, give us a song,' she was saying.

'*No!*' Frank thought.

'No, I don't think so,' Guy said.

'Oh, go on,' said Jackie. 'I like a good tune.'

This was all Frank needed. Once Guy started playing the guitar there was no stopping him. They'd be there all night. He focused all his attention on Guy, and to his surprise Guy was blushing and looking pleased. But he shook his head.

'Some other time,' he said.

Jackie came over to Frank's cage again.

'You'll have to take good care of this little fella,' she said.

Guy had spoken about Jackie before – he knew her from the Angel, where she worked two evenings a week and Sunday lunch-times – but Frank hadn't really listened. Now a new thought occurred to him, 'Did Guy *like* Jackie?'

Frank looked hard at her. He supposed she did have quite a nice face for a human – not as bristly as Guy's, but sleek and brown. And a dark shiny tail, though it was in a funny place for a tail, swinging from the top of her head. He supposed it was possible that Guy did like Jackie, but it wasn't an entirely pleasant thought, since Frank certainly didn't want any contact with Jake and Josh.

Guy squatted beside Jackie and both their faces loomed over Frank.

'It's amazing when you think,' he said, 'that they come all the way from the deserts of Syria but they adapt to living in little cages in our front rooms.'

'My dad came from Syria,' Jackie said, 'but I never really knew him.'

Frank pricked up his ears at this, but Jackie and Guy didn't tell him anything useful – about how to get there, or what it was like – they just started talking about families, and settling in other countries. And all Frank really wanted to think about was rescuing Elsie and George, and Mabel. Then Jackie extended her finger towards Frank and stroked him quickly before he could move.

'I suppose he's company for you,' she said, standing up. 'You need someone to talk to if you don't have a job. I'd go mad without my jobs.' Then she said, 'You know what, we're looking for someone to be a lollipop lady – or man – near the school – that crossing's terrible.'

Guy didn't understand at first, but when he did, the look on his face was quite comical.

'*Me?*' he said.

'Well, it's only part-time,' said Jackie. 'It'd leave you plenty of time for your music. And you'd be doing something really valuable –'

'But I want to be a hardcore, tectonic, riff-sizzlin' guitar hero,' said Guy. 'Not a lollipop man!'

Jackie looked mildly offended.

'Well, it was only a thought,' she said. She picked up her jacket. 'I'd better be going. The kids are at Khalid's and I said I'd pick them up. And I expect you'll want to, er, tidy up.'

She picked up some chip paper that was lying on the rug, and handed Guy a plate that was peeping out from under the settee. Guy opened the door.

'Let me know if you change your mind,' Jackie said over her shoulder as she left.

'Lollipop man!' said Guy crossly, putting the plate back under the settee. 'Where is she coming from?' He scattered the chip paper back over the rug. 'Lollipop man!'

If Frank hadn't been so worried he might have smiled. As it was, he was too busy trying to think of a Plan of Action. The first thing that was clear was that he had to get out of his cage. This wasn't as simple as it used to be, since each time Frank had escaped Guy had tried harder to make his cage secure – first with string, then wire (forgetting that what hamsters do best is gnaw) and now with a little padlock. Frank had objected strongly to this and had tried to command Guy not to do it, but Guy had been determined.

'It's for your own good, Frank,' he'd said. 'What if you wander off one day and don't come back?'

Of course, this was exactly what Frank was hoping to do, but on this point Guy would not be budged. The best Frank could do was to make him forget to put the padlock on, which was moderately easy, especially if Guy had been drinking lager with his cheese and chutney sandwiches.

Tonight, however, Guy was obviously not going to forget the padlock. He checked it three times in fact, and even then he couldn't seem to settle. And Frank couldn't even begin to escape until Guy went upstairs and left him alone.

'I'm not leaving you alone tonight, Frank,' Guy said. 'I'm going to sleep down here with you.'

'Great,' Frank thought.

He waited impatiently for Guy to fall asleep on

the settee, but Guy was still restless. He kept getting up and checking the doors and windows, and muttering about what he'd do if he caught anyone trying to break in.

'*Lie down*,' Frank told him, and eventually Guy did. But not before finding an old cricket bat and testing his swing several times.

'Anyone comes after you, Frank,' he said, 'has to get past me first.'

Frank sighed. This was all very well, but it was hardly helping him rescue Elsie, Mabel or George. 'Poor Elsie,' he thought again, and 'Poor George,' and even (though he didn't like her very much) 'Poor Mabel!' Who knew for what dreadful reason they'd been taken? Frank couldn't even begin to think what horrid plans the thief might have. But he did know one thing: he, Frank, was going to stop him. His pelt had lifted, his blood was up. That thief was going to be *very sorry* he had taken Frank's friends. Frank would make him sorry as soon as he found him. That was the first thing he had to do.

But how?

All Frank could think was that once he was out of his cage he would make his way to Elsie, George and Mabel's homes and try to pick up the trail. That was the best idea he could come up with, and it was as far as he'd got. The thief might be anywhere by now; he might have driven them all away in a van.

But it was a start, and sometimes that's all you need. That, and some Courage! of course. And Frank did have a cunning plan for getting out of his cage. He reckoned that he could separate the steel framework of his cage from the tray at the bottom if he pushed and rattled hard enough. That was going to be hard with Guy in the room. But as soon as he fell asleep Frank was going to try.

While he was waiting, Frank busied himself packing his pouches for the journey. This is what he packed:

Some cheese and chutney (he didn't like chutney, but it was hard to separate it from the cheese).

A few sunflower seeds.

A bit of husk from the hamster food.

Some peanuts Guy had brought home from the pub.

A nice chunk of carrot.

He debated for a while about whether or not to pack his bedding, since he didn't know when he'd be back, and it sometimes got cold in the Spaces Between. It was actually possible to stuff his entire bed into his pouches, but that made his pouches enormous and it would be difficult to squeeze through the smaller chinks and crannies if he carried too much with him. Besides, if Guy caught him stuffing his bed into his pouches he might get suspicious, and that was the last thing Frank wanted. So in the end he contented himself with making sure that he had a good long drink of water – more than he felt he needed – because the Spaces Between were very dry and dusty, and thirst could be more of a problem than hunger. And he spent some time limbering up for the journey on his wheel.

Finally, Guy did fall asleep. His head lolled backwards off the edge of the settee and his mouth dropped open rather unattractively, and he was soon snoring loudly enough to cover some of the noise Frank made, so Frank was able to set to work.

First, he tugged with his teeth at the bottom prongs that kept the steel frame attached to the tray, then he pushed his nose upwards through the bars and rattled them furiously, and then he tugged upwards with his paws.

It was hard work. The first prong wouldn't budge at all, and the next one shifted but didn't give. From time to time a bar made a loud twanging noise as it sprang back into place, and Frank held his breath, but, although Guy shifted and mumbled, he didn't wake up.

Frank went around his cage, tugging all the prongs. Finally, the next to last one gave, and when Frank tugged and rattled the next one to it, the whole cage sprang apart!

There was a terrific clatter and a shower of wood-shavings flew up. Frank sneezed, and for a moment it looked as though Guy might roll right off the settee. Frank held his breath, then scrambled over the rim of his cage and under the steel bars, which were now askew. Although Guy half sat up, he rolled the other way, still asleep, with his nose pressed into the cushions of the settee. Vastly relieved, Frank ran along the ledge on which his cage stood.

This ledge was very useful to Frank. It stood about a foot away from the floor and ran the full length of one wall beneath the gas fire, which stuck out from the wall just a few inches higher than the ledge. It had been built by the people who had lived at number 13 before Guy, and it was very ugly, Guy said, being covered in slate. He had always intended to do something about it, but of course he hadn't got around to it. Frank didn't want him to get around to it, because the ledge was something of a gift. It was easy to jump from it on to the carpet, and to climb back up, and by running along it Frank had access to most of the room. Best of all, where it ran beneath the gas fire, there was a gap in the slates, and by dropping down through it Frank could get into the Spaces Between.

Even though by now it was a familiar experience, Frank always felt a thrill at the moment when the ledge fell away and there was only the plunge into the musty, dusty darkness. He dropped on to a wooden ledge, then down again on to the Floor Beneath the Floor. This was covered with all kinds of fine rubble, loose slate and brick dust, and other interesting objects, like mouse droppings, and drawing pins and screws. Each time Frank came here, it seemed that there was something new and interesting to explore, and it was very tempting to stay for a while and investigate all the strange sounds and smells, the taps and gurgles and muffled clicks that echo through the Spaces Between. But Frank was on a mission, so there wasn't time.

Below ground all Frank's deepest, oldest instincts were surfacing, and now he had to channel them into his Quest.

Frank reared on to his hind legs, pricked his ears

and sniffed. He could smell his own scent from all the occasions he had travelled through the Spaces Between. The main joist was at his side. This was a long beam of wood that ran beneath the floors of all the houses. If he followed it he would come to Mabel's house first, then to the house where there were no animals at all, and a house where all the cats lived, and then to George's house, and Elsie's. If he hadn't picked up a trail by then he didn't know what he would do, but he still didn't have any other ideas.

He couldn't help thinking that now might be a good time for the Black Hamster to return and tell him what to do. It was here, in the space beneath Guy's house, that Frank had first heard his Call. It seemed like a long time ago. 'If only he would return,' Frank thought, and he had a brief, lovely vision of the two of them working together to rescue Frank's friends.

But there was no Call; no scent or sign of anything but the old, forgotten dust and debris of the house and a whiff of drains. Pushing aside a slight sense of disappointment, Frank set off, running along the length of the joist.

Where it left one house and entered another, the joist was surrounded by a brick wall. But there were always chinks and gaps between the bricks where the mortar had come loose. Hamsters can squeeze through the smallest spaces, so Frank pushed and wriggled and kicked his way through to the space beneath the floor of the house where Mabel lived.

Frank followed the scent of Mabel, the scent of a fine, proud hamster who thought very highly of herself, and soon picked up another scent that didn't belong to any of the Wheelers. It was the scent of strange human, mixed with the smell of leather and cigarettes. He followed this all the way from beneath the floor of the lounge to beneath the floor of the kitchen, and from there to the back wall of the house.

There he paused. He could tell that the thief had left by the back door. Frank was familiar with the front of the house, where there was a road, and across the road was the Wild. But he didn't know what was at the back at all, except for the cats at number 7, and they were definitely to be avoided. It might still be best, he thought, to visit Elsie and George's houses first, just to check that the trails all led the same way, before dashing off into unknown territory.

Frank rubbed his paws over his face a few times. He was sweating from his exertions. He wasn't as fit as he should be. He had started to get used to a comfortable life recently, and hadn't kept up his programme of exercises. He had even stopped running round his wheel. How would he manage if he had to travel for miles beneath busy roads? He didn't know. But the thought of Elsie and George and even Mabel being frightened or hurt was unbearable to him. He had to be up to the task ahead. He had to find them.

'Courage!' he murmured to himself.

Almost immediately, something happened.

It was as though the darkness in front of him was peeling away.

Frank blinked, and stared.

He was staring, not at bricks and joist, but at a rocky passage, leading away into the darkness.

Frank blinked again and the vision disappeared.

He took a step forward in the darkness, then two or three more.

He thought he could see it again, ahead of him, a faint, sandy-coloured glow.

It couldn't be – but yes, there it was.

Was he seeing things? Frank didn't know, but he intended to find out. He stepped forward. There it was again, definitely closer, and now he could see something moving.

On Frank went, and the further he travelled, the stranger the experience became. On one level, he knew he was travelling through the Spaces Between, following the long joists and scrambling through holes in the bricks. On another level, he felt that he was travelling through sand and stone, past strange and beautiful rock formations, towards a mysterious cavern, where he could faintly see the shadowy forms of hamsters. Hundreds and thousands of hamsters, all moving rhythmically, in a mysterious dance.

While running towards the hamsters in this vision, Frank passed beneath Arthur and Jean's house, and the house of Mrs Timms, where he smelled the sharp, sour scent of cat wee and alcohol, and George's house, where he could smell Jackie, and the scent of young humans, and their cat. Here the scent of Intruder was powerful again, as it was beneath Elsie's house, but all the time, as though watching a different channel on TV, he was following the rocky path towards the cavern, and the dancing hamsters. His nostrils were full of the smell of desert, and the ancient scents of his tribe. His blood hummed through his veins, he felt powerful, and keenly alive, and another, peculiar sensation, as though he was returning home.

Frank knew he had to stay focused on the job in hand – on rescuing Elsie, Mabel and George – yet in his vision he experienced another, older Call, to leave his life of captivity on Bright Street and to return to his tribe. As he ran faster and faster through the Spaces Between it was no longer clear to him where he was going, which Call he was answering, or the true nature of his Quest.

Then, as suddenly as it had begun, the vision ended. The desert, the dancing hamsters and the cavern all vanished as though snuffed out like a candle flame. Frank was left facing a brick wall.

Frank ran about for a few moments, searching and sniffing, then finally he stood still, mystified. A thin draught of air came through a chink in the brickwork. Where was he? And where had all the hamsters gone?

Only one thing was clear, as he stood in the cold musty darkness. The scent of hamster hadn't disappeared, in fact it was quite overpowering. And he could still smell the leather and cigarettes. And mingled with both scents was the smell of something much worse, the smell of some horror that Frank had never encountered before, but which was so strong that he staggered and retched. There was blood in the smell, and chemicals Frank couldn't name, and fear, and doom.

Frank's pelt bristled all over. He could hardly bear to breathe. Had he been lured, finally, to the Pits of Doom? And if he had, what on earth could he do about it? Should he try to run back the way he had come? In his confusion, he could hardly remember the way. But, in any case, what about Elsie and Mabel, and George?

Slowly an awful thought penetrated Frank's anxiety. Suppose the blood he could smell was his friends'?

He had to stay calm, and think.

Whatever the smell was, it was coming through the chink in the bricks. He closed his eyes, and made himself sniff. He couldn't actually smell Elsie, Mabel or George, which calmed him a little. He tried to think clearly. Where was he?

It took Frank a moment or two to work out that he had come to the dividing wall between Elsie's house, which was number 3, and number 1, the house which stood empty for most of the year but which was rented out from time to time by the owner, Mr Marusiak.

A man was renting it at the moment, but no one seemed to know anything about him. He didn't seem to go out much, and he kept the curtains drawn in the daytime. Guy had told Frank that he had met him once and tried to be friendly, but the man didn't seem the friendly type. He lived on his own, and had no visitors. Mr Marusiak didn't allow pets.

Why would there be such a strong scent of hamster from the rented house?

Nose quivering and senses alert, Frank suddenly knew that he had been led here by his vision. *This* was the place. The hamsters were here, and he had been brought here to rescue them!

Frank didn't waste any time. Forgetting his fear, and the horror, forgetting even his vision of the desert hamsters, he launched himself at the chink in the mortar between the bricks, clawing and nibbling it. As soon as the chink widened, he thrust himself into it, kicking furiously. He was so excited at the prospect of saving lost hamsters that he didn't even notice he wasn't going the usual way. Instead of making his way upwards through the chink to the skirting board, and emerging into the living room of number 1, he was actually travelling downwards, following the terrible scent. And when his nose finally emerged, through mortar and a layer of plaster, instead of carpet or floor-boards all he could sense was a huge, dizzying drop.

Yes, alone of all the houses on Bright Street, number 1 had a cellar, a Room Beneath.

For a moment Frank was too shocked to move, which was just as well, for he would certainly have fallen from an alarming height. Sickened by the foul smell, he thought, just for a moment, of retreat. Then he muttered his motto again, 'Courage!', in case there were any further visions.

Nothing happened.

But now he was sure he could detect, mingled with the sickening smells, the familiar smells of Elsie, George and Mabel. So he *couldn't* go back. However, he couldn't see how he could go forward.

High up on the wall to his left there was a tiny grille. A sliver of moonlight came through it, and as Frank's eyes adjusted he could make out a small cluttered room with peeling plaster on the walls. There were tins and boxes everywhere, of different shapes and sizes, some of them with the lids not properly fastened down. These were exuding horrible smells.

Directly below the grille there was an old sink, with some tins stacked up beside it. There was also a long table, like the kind that Guy had used when he had decided to decorate, and on this there were more tins, and some large, mysterious object covered by a thick plastic sheet. To the right of the table there were stone steps leading up to a door. As Frank gazed slowly around the room he could make out shelves with yet more tins on them. There was a hook on the wall below him, and a line stretched from it to another hook on the wall to his right.

The next thing he saw froze the marrow in his bones and sent a sensation like wind whistling through the spaces in his head. Pegged to the line, like some macabre Christmas decoration, was a long row of hamster skins.

5 Trapped

Horrified, Frank retreated. He scrambled and kicked his way backwards along the chink until he was back in the Spaces Between. There he paused, resting one paw on the bricks for support. He was sick to his stomach and chilled to the bone. He couldn't even take it in properly. But he knew now that the worst of all the bad smells was the smell of death.

Frank had never smelled death before, but he knew it by instinct, as surely as if he'd been raised in a cemetery. He should have known it before, when he had first smelled the air through the chink, but he hadn't wanted to know. Now that he did know, he felt a burst of anguish for Elsie, George, and even Mabel, who had never been very nice.

But maybe they weren't dead yet. They might be trapped somewhere – imprisoned and afraid. Frank had to find out. Because, from what he had just seen, if they weren't dead yet, they soon would be.

But how could he find out?

He had to go back. Back into the room of horror, the Chamber of Fear.

Frank felt as though his stomach and all his bones

had turned to water. 'Where were the Desert Hamsters?' he thought. 'Where was the Black Hamster when you needed him?' Frank licked his lips nervously, then peered into the darkness, hoping to catch sight of someone, anyone who might help. But there was nothing, and no one.

If ever Frank needed his motto, it was now.

'Courage,' he told himself weakly, then, 'Courage, courage.'

And as he repeated his motto he thought he could feel a tiny flame ignite somewhere inside him, very faint and far away, like a star.

'Think,' he told himself. 'And sniff.'

Steeling himself against the smell of death, Frank sniffed long and hard at the chink in the wall, and at the ghastly bouquet of blood and fear that came through it. Beyond the chink, faint and far away, he was sure he could detect a scent of living hamster and even – though he didn't know if this was only because he wanted it so much – a faraway whiff of Elsie, Mabel and George. If they were alive, somewhere in this terrible house, it was Frank's job to find them. He stood back and began to look for another point of entry.

In all houses there are cracks and chinks that humans can barely see, which are doorways for hamsters into passages through which they can travel for miles. Frank ran beneath one joist then another, searching and sniffing. Then he clambered on top of a joist, sneezing because of all the dust.

Nothing. Not even the smallest chink. There was

only the crack leading him back into that dreadful Room Beneath.

He had to go back in, to explore it and see if other hamsters were trapped there. And perhaps, once he was there, he could make his way into the rest of the house.

Pushing himself back into that crack was the hardest thing Frank had ever done. He wriggled and squirmed, trying not to breathe too much or to think. When at last he peeped out again at the small, cluttered room, he could see that there were lots of ways of getting around it – a stack of tins here, a wooden crate there, a ladder propped up against the wall near the sink. And directly below him, but a considerable drop away, there was a shelf running along the length of the wall.

Frank peered into the darkness, trying to make out the different bumpy shapes on the shelf. He reckoned that the distance to the shelf itself was more than the height of three hamsters. But a little to his left there was a large tin. If he jumped that way, instead of just dropping, he might land on it. He had to hope that the lid was on.

Frank levered himself out of the crack as far as he dared, feeling his way down the rough plaster on the walls. When he had got as far as he could, he closed his eyes, took a breath and pushed himself away from the wall in what he hoped was the direction of the tin.

Meanwhile, Elsie was gradually growing accustomed to her new abode. There were things she didn't like about it, especially the air, which was drenched with a sickly, heavy smell that masked everything else. But from the point of view of comfort she couldn't complain. It was warm, and there was always a vast abundance of good food. Their new Owner came in twice a day to feed them, and he always piled their food bowls high. He didn't talk to them much, or play, but he always came with food, and soon Elsie got used to the smell of him and forgot to be nervous or wary.

And she got to know the other hamsters, though she did still think it was a bit strange, them all being kept together like this. It was strange that no one answered when she mentioned the empty cages, but then, most of the time they were all so drowsy. Daisy was still lively, and cheeky. She called Elsie 'Old Bossy-Boots' and always interrupted when she was talking to George. And she was always showing off, swinging from the bars of her cage, running backwards and forwards on the wheel. 'Can you do this, can you do this?' she would cry constantly, whenever it looked like George was paying attention to Elsie.

It was during one of her many acrobatic displays that Elsie first noticed that Daisy had a club-foot – or, rather, that one of her hind paws ended in a stump. George didn't seem to have noticed this. He was very taken with Daisy. Often when Elsie woke up they were already deep in conversation or playing together, though they were in separate cages, by mirroring each other: George would kick up some wood-shavings, Daisy would kick up some wood-shavings; Daisy would climb four bars of her cage, and George would climb four of his, and so on.

Elsie didn't approve at all. She thought Daisy was not good enough for George and, besides, secretly, she felt a bit neglected. After all, the only good thing about being brought to this strange place was that George was here. But there was no time to catch up on everything that had happened since the last time they were together, because Daisy never gave them the chance.

'What about this?' she would say, swinging upside-down from her bars.

On one of these occasions, Elsie got quite cross.

'I suppose that's why nobody ever bought you

from the pet shop,' she said waspishly. 'Because you're lame.'

There was a shocked silence.

Mabel stopped eating.

George looked horrified.

For a hamster to draw attention to a wound or disability in another hamster is the worst breech of etiquette. Even Elsie was shocked by what she had said. Daisy looked mortified. She went very quiet and retreated to the back of her cage. Elsie turned her back, ashamed of herself, then went to hide in her bedding. But she didn't apologize.

'I've said it now,' she told herself. 'It can't be unsaid.'

She curled herself up and shed a quiet tear. But the next time she woke up Daisy was back to normal, bouncing and swinging around as if nothing had happened. Elsie could see that this was her way of coping with her damaged leg – to try even harder to do extraordinary things – but she still didn't like her. And she couldn't see what George saw in her at all.

It was the same with Maurice and Mabel. Maurice openly declared his adoration of Mabel. He admired everything she said, laughed far too loudly at her jokes, and greeted her with praise every evening when she got up.

'Oh my snow-white queen!' he would say as she opened her eyes. 'How can I serve you today?'

Mabel would look at him balefully through one half-open eye.

'Not you again,' she would say. 'Don't you ever go to sleep?'

But none of this had any effect. Maurice worshipped Mabel and Mabel let him. She had even worked out a system whereby Maurice could pass his food to her. Maurice had a straw in his cage and he could fire small pellets of food through it towards Mabel's cage. Then, when the Owner came in, he would scoop up the food near Mabel's cage and put it into her food bowl.

The worst thing was that the Owner seemed to think Mabel was special too. She was the only one he spoke to or handled. He would take her out of her cage and examine her carefully.

'Yes, what a beauty,' he'd say. 'Look at the shine on that coat.' And he always gave her extra food.

None of this was very good for Mabel, of course. When she wasn't eating, she spent her entire time preening herself, to the accompaniment of more flattery from Maurice.

'That's right, my angel, comb out those wondrous whiskers.' 'Does my swan-queen need a nut to sharpen her splendid incisors?' and so on, in quite a sickening way.

Elsie would often look rather wistfully at Felicity with Drew. Felicity was always grooming him or teaching him to groom himself, and monitoring his diet. Drew didn't always appreciate this, needless to say.

'Oh *Mum*,' he'd say as she cleaned his ears or made him check his food for droppings. 'Not *again*.'

But Felicity insisted on showing him how to pack

his pouches in the most efficient way, to use his scent glands to mark his territory, to make a bed from raw materials, and how to insulate it properly against cold and damp.

She was so busy instructing Drew that she hardly had time to talk to anyone else, let alone Elsie.

'Why couldn't I have had a mother like that?' she thought, looking darkly at Mabel, who was stuffing herself as usual.

The one hamster who did talk to Elsie was Chestnut. He was getting on in years and had a lot to tell – stories of all the other hamsters who'd come and gone in the pet shop.

'There was one called Abby. A little beauty, no bigger than yourself, all black and brown. Twenty young she had, *twenty*. What a sight that was! You couldn't hardly see her when they was all feeding. They all found good homes though ... You should have seen Mitch. What a fighter! Even took on a rabbit ...'

Elsie liked Chestnut and she enjoyed hearing all his stories, though often he would trail off before the end as though he couldn't quite remember – and go back to sleep. Still, when he was awake he was good company and she was always pleased to see his friendly face. She couldn't help wondering why he hadn't found an Owner before now.

'I always thought of Mr Wiggs as my Owner,' he said once. 'We was good friends, me and Old Wiggsy. He always had a special treat for me. "Chestnut," he'd say, "other hamsters come and go, but you're still here." Of course this new Owner, he brings us things too, but it's not the same,' he said with a sigh. 'It's not the same.'

Elsie knew exactly what Chestnut meant. She couldn't forget Lucy, and couldn't help wondering if she would ever see her again. Was Lucy missing her? Elsie thought about Lucy before she went to sleep, and whenever she woke up she thought for just one moment that she was in her real home. But in between the memories faded. It was so warm, and there was so much food and such a heavy scent that it was hard to think clearly, or even to stay awake. Nothing much happened. The new Owner came and went. Every evening he watched telly and ate chips, then before he went to bed he re-lit the smoking sticks and oil burners that released their heavy vapours into the room, and left the fire burning low. And time passed in a warm glow, with all the hamsters eating and sleeping, and soon it was hard to remember that there had ever been a time of not being here.

One evening 'Uncle Vince', as he insisted on calling himself, went out as usual for his chips. Elsie cast a drowsy eye around the room. It was the time when hamsters usually got up and started being active. But they had all just eaten another huge meal, and even Daisy seemed barely able to move. Mabel lay on her back, her stomach so rounded it looked as though she might be having another litter of cubs. Drew lay curled up next to Felicity, who licked him from time to time in a half-hearted way. George and Maurice were asleep – Maurice had fallen asleep watching Mabel, propped up against the bars of his cage. Chestnut stared dully at the wall, murmuring, 'I wonder what old Wiggsy's doing now,' from time to time, or 'It's not the same.'

Elsie felt that something wasn't right. Surely they should all be more active than this? But she felt too sleepy to work it out. She was about to close her eyes and slide again into a heavy doze, when something caught her eye. Something was squeezing itself through the gap where the door hadn't been quite closed.

Elsie was as short-sighted as the rest of her race and from where she was it looked like a small, brownish blur. She watched it struggle without feeling particularly nervous or wary, only a kind of melancholy interest.

'Perhaps it's a dream,' she thought.

Then the blur shook itself and stood up, sniffing. Something wrinkled the surface of Elsie's memory, a different scent penetrated the powerful fragrance in the room.

'Why, it's Frank,' she said slowly. Then, 'George, look, it's Frank!'

George didn't move.

'Elsie?' Frank said. 'Elsie! I've found you!'

Frank noticed a small table with complicated woodwork round the legs in the middle of the room. It looked as if it would be easy to climb. He ran up it quickly and stood in the centre of it. Meanwhile Elsie was trying to wake up the others.

'George, George! It's Frank! Chestnut, Felicity, this is my friend Frank!'

But the only response she had was from Mabel, who opened one eye and said, 'Well, well, if it isn't the little squeaker himself,' then closed it again.

'Oh Frank,' said Elsie. 'However did you get here?'

'Never mind that,' said Frank. 'The point is, you've all got to come with me right now.'

From the back of the room came a lazy drawl.

'And why, pray, would we want to do that?'

It was Maurice, who had woken up and was watching Frank suspiciously.

Frank was hoping that he wouldn't have to go into too much detail about the horrifying things he'd seen.

'You're all in terrible danger,' he said.

Elsie didn't know what to say to this, but Chestnut opened his eyes and said slowly, 'Excuse me, young chap, I don't know who you are, but you can't just barge in here and expect us all to follow you just like that. Did Uncle Vince bring you here?'

'Uncle who?' said Frank.

Mabel was more awake now, watching Frank with lazy amusement.

'You don't want to listen to him,' she said to Chestnut. 'He'll have you all looking for the Black Hamster – in the Pits of Doom.'

This caused a general stir and even George woke up.

'Frank?' he said. 'It is you! Oh I am glad. Now we're all here together.' He beamed at Daisy. 'It's Frank,' he said.

Daisy glanced dismissively at Frank.

'He's cute,' she said. 'But not as cute as you, Georgie-baby.'

George's ears went pink.

'Hee hee hee,' he said.

Frank shook himself. This was all wrong. He wasn't getting through. And what was wrong with the scent in this room? It was heavy, and sickening, so powerful he could hardly think. He tried again.

'Listen to me,' he said. 'I don't know who this Uncle Vince is, but I do know that he's got you all here for a reason. You mustn't trust him. You've got to get out. I can get you out. You've got to follow me.'

'Follow you where?' said Felicity.

'To the Pits of Doom, of course,' said Mabel, and Maurice laughed unpleasantly.

Chestnut said, 'Now look here, young chap, this is all very well, but we don't know you, and you say that we've not got to trust Uncle Vince and we've got to trust you – well – it's a bit much.'

'We know him,' Elsie said. 'Tell them, George.'

'Frank's our friend,' George said. 'But, Frank, we're all happy here. We don't want to leave. Why don't you stay?'

'It's great here,' said Daisy.

'Absolute luxury,' said Maurice.

'We love being here,' they all said with one voice, except for Elsie, but she looked too dazed and dull to say anything else.

Frank stared around the room at the hamsters and the empty hamster cages. This was weird. There was something, well, *spooky* about it all. Had the man who'd burgled all the houses, the monster who'd done horrible deeds in the Room Beneath, got them all hypnotized? Why wasn't he getting through? Frank tried again.

'Why do you think he's got all of you here together?' he said. 'And what about your Owners? Don't you think they've been worried. I've been worried.'

But Daisy and Chestnut said, 'We're from the pet shop.'

And George said, 'I don't know about everyone else, but I'm having a better time here.'

And Mabel said, 'This Owner knows how to treat a hamster.'

'Perhaps he wants to breed more of us,' Felicity modestly suggested, cuddling Drew, and Maurice smiled hungrily at Mabel.

'We like it here,' they all said, eerily.

'Elsie?' Frank said.

Elsie paused, a little troubled.

'It's sweet of you to worry, Frank. We were all worried at first. But, really, this new place couldn't be nicer. I know our Owners will miss us,' she said, thinking with a pang about Lucy, 'but they'll probably get new pets. And we're all warm, and the food's wonderful, and, well, I do like being with George.'

George smiled lovingly at Elsie.

Frank looked at all the empty cages.

'What about them?' he said. 'What happened to all the other hamsters?'

There was a pause, before everyone started talking at once.

'We think he found them new homes.'

'Gave them as presents to friends.'

'He's kept the *special* ones, of course. He called me a real find.'

'And so you are, my pumpkin seed,' said Maurice. 'He knows a good thing when he sees it.'

Frank tried again. 'You don't know this man. You don't know what he's done. But if you come with me, I'll show you.'

'Now, look here,' Chestnut said again. 'You say we've all got to follow you, but where exactly? And how are we supposed to get out?'

'I can get you out,' Frank said. 'We have to go down ... there's a kind of ... room ... beneath the ground. And a sink. We can get out through a pipe ... into the sewer ... and away from this house. But we've got to go *now*.'

As he spoke, his own words sounded hollow and unconvincing in this dream-like atmosphere. Mabel gave a little snort of laughter.

'Well there you have it,' she said. 'There's your choice. You can stay here – with all this lovely grub, and be warm and clean and safe – or you can follow a mad hamster into a *sewer* –' she wrinkled her nose in distaste – 'and let him take you straight to the Pits of Doom. Well, I don't know, hmm, what shall I choose?'

Maurice laughed and Chestnut frowned.

Frank glared at them all in despair. He was beginning to get angry. It looked as though he was going to have to tell them about the Chamber of Fear. But would they believe him? He closed his eyes. The heavy sweet smell was all around him, but beneath it, still powerful in his nostrils, was the sickening smell of fear and death. What was the matter with them all? Couldn't *they* smell it? Or didn't they want to know? He tried again.

'I know what happened to the other hamsters,' he said. 'Open your senses! Wake up and sniff the air! Can't you smell it?'

Everyone looked puzzled, or suspicious.

'Smell what?'

'I can't smell anything.'

'Nose too near his own scent glands if you ask me.'

'I used to think it smelled a bit funny when I got here,' George said slowly. 'But now I'm used to it, it's quite nice really. Sort of relaxing. And it hides all the other smells.'

The other hamsters agreed.

Frank stamped his paw. 'That's the point!' he shouted. 'Exactly! Someone's trying to hide the other smells.'

'What smells?' said Mabel. 'The only funny smell in here is you. Sewers indeed!'

And little Drew said, 'Who is that hamster, Mum? I don't like him. Make him go away.'

Frank stared at them in despair. It was no good. He knew from his own experience that life in captivity tended to dull the senses, to make even the keenest hamster stupid and slow, but this was beyond anything he had ever encountered before. All these hamsters, flatly denying they could smell anything, when the room reeked of a sweet perfume and death! What was he going to do?

'You're all in terrible danger,' he said again. 'That's what I'm trying to tell you. You have to follow me – or you'll all die.'

There was a shocked silence. Then one small voice spoke.

'Well, I don't think Frank would make up anything like this. If he says there's danger, we should listen.'

It was Elsie. Frank looked at her gratefully, but Mabel said, 'Tosh, he just can't bear to see other hamsters being happy.'

Now Frank was really angry. His fur bristled and he bared his teeth. But just at that moment, all the hamsters heard footsteps outside. And the next moment there was the sound of a key turning in the lock.

'Frank, quick!' Elsie squeaked.

She didn't know why she said it – after all, Uncle Vince *loved* hamsters, but she suddenly felt a terrible danger.

Frank had already run back down the carved legs of the table, and he had just whisked himself behind the armchair when big footsteps clumped across the room, making the furniture and all the hamster cages rattle.

Once more Frank picked up the scent of leather and cigarettes, much more powerfully this time. It was mingled with another smell that Frank recognized from living with Guy – this human had been to the pub. And he had bought chips on the way home. He walked towards the hamster cages and spoke in a big, rasping voice.

'Hello, my beauties,' he said. 'How are you doing? Come and say hello to Uncle Vince.'

Frank's pelt quivered as Vince put his hand in the cages and petted the hamsters. Only Elsie held back a little, the others seemed quite happy to be handled, especially when Vince started sharing out his chips.

'He's the Enemy,' Frank thought. 'Why can't they smell it?'

'Now, I want you to eat up all this lovely food,' Vince went on, filling their bowls. 'Make you grow nice and plump. Makes your coats lovely – thick and glossy, oh yes.'

Frank's coat bristled with fury.

'I want you all fattened up lovely like this one,' Vince said, stroking Mabel. 'All sleek and shiny.'

Mabel preened.

After checking all the cages Vince finally sat down in the armchair behind which Frank was hiding. He opened a can of beer.

Now, what was Frank going to do? He could hardly start liberating hamsters with Vince in the room, and he knew from his experiences with Guy that once a big human settled in an armchair with a can of beer, it might be hours before he moved.

His only hope was that he might fall asleep, as Guy often did. And then Frank would have to start all over again, trying to convince the hamsters to go with him, when they clearly wanted to stay here, with Uncle Vince.

Somehow, he would have to make them see that they were in danger.

They wouldn't believe him, they had to see it for themselves.

It was then that Frank had his idea.

'But it probably wouldn't work,' he thought, closing his eyes. He'd had no evidence that it did work, except on Guy.

'Please,' he thought, 'I *need* it to work,' and he groped in his thoughts for some point of contact with Uncle Vince's mind.

At first there was only darkness. Uncle Vince put his feet on the table and opened another can.

'Please,' Frank thought again, straining all the nerves in his body towards this one end – to establishing the same contact he had with Guy. He concentrated hard, gripping strands of carpet in his paws.

Suddenly the thought came to him out of

nowhere that Uncle Vince was relaxing now and that Frank too should relax.

'Let it flow,' the thought said.

Frank relaxed. Breathing more deeply, he stopped concentrating on Uncle Vince and became aware instead of the power he had been trying to use. It returned to him, as he breathed in and out, and wove itself round him in a kind of silvery light. And suddenly it seemed to him that he could hear the burglar's thoughts, a nasty jumble of money and beer.

Frank gathered the silvery light about him and breathed it in. Then he spoke into the centre of Uncle Vince's thoughts.

'Speak your intentions,' he told Uncle Vince. 'Tell them what you plan to do.'

For a moment nothing happened. Uncle Vince took a long swig of beer. Frank went on breathing and focusing his thoughts on the silvery light, his intentions on Uncle Vince.

Suddenly Uncle Vince began to hum, a big deep hum like a giant bee. He hummed the tune of 'Sing a Song of Sixpence', then broke into these words:

'Four and twenty ham-sters
Pegged out on a line . . .'

There was an alarmed stirring from the cages.

'When the skins are hanging
Strung out in a row
I'll tack them all together
And then begin to sew . . .'

'Oh, sorry,' Vince said, rolling a bleary eye in the direction of the hamsters, who by now seemed very agitated indeed. 'I forgot you was all listening. Still, you had to find out sometime. And you know, you can't keep your skins forever. Sooner or later you snuff it – sooner, being hamsters – and then what happens to all them beautiful pelts? They rot away, that's what.' He shook his head. 'Such a waste. Whereas this way they get to be preserved in mint condition. So it's much better to pop your clogs now, while they're still prime. Listen to me.' Uncle Vince chuckled as the hamsters all stared at him in horror. 'I'm talking just as if you could understand.' He shook his head again, still chuckling. 'Just as well you can't, eh?' and he winked at them broadly and settled further into the armchair.

This was more than Frank had hoped for. When he peeped out from behind the chair he could see that the hamsters were visibly shaken. Chestnut was clutching his heart and murmuring, 'Oh dear, oh dear!' Felicity was hugging Drew, and Maurice had hidden at the back of his cage. George looked outraged, Elsie looked worried almost to tears and Daisy had stopped mid-swing, still clinging to the bars of her cage. Even Mabel looked shocked.

Frank could feel the silvery light withdrawing, to

the size of a kernel, then a speck, his access to Uncle Vince's mind closed. Just at that moment the burglar's hand, still holding the can of beer, drooped, and he began to snore.

Frank waited a moment for the snoring to settle into a regular rhythm before he ran back up the table legs and stood next to Uncle Vince's feet.

'Well?' he said. '*Now* will you come with me?'

There was a satisfying chorus of 'Get us out of here!' and 'Oh, please hurry – quick!' and 'I can't believe it, I just can't believe it!'

Only Mabel said, 'I *don't* believe it, it's a trick!'

Frank stared at her. '*What?*' he said.

'Hypnotism,' Mabel said. 'Or ventriloquism. Whatever.'

Frank opened his mouth to speak, but changed his mind. There wasn't any time. Already the hamsters were rattling the doors of their cages, which had been fastened with tape for extra security.

Frank ran up the back of the armchair to get to the bureau where Chestnut's cage was. Once he had freed Chestnut, the elderly hamster ran gamely to Maurice's cage and began chewing through the tape, while Frank concentrated on Elsie and George.

'Stock up on food,' he told them. 'Fill your pouches now.'

Some of the hamsters weren't very used to climbing down furniture. George helped Daisy, Elsie helped Felicity and Drew and Frank helped Chestnut. Maurice clung to the edge of the bureau and practically had to be carried down by Frank, though he was quite young and able-bodied. Then he whimpered and complained whenever Frank slipped.

Frank left Mabel till last, mainly because she had annoyed him. She pretended to ignore them all, eating her food casually, but Frank caught her watching once or twice.

'She doesn't know what to do,' he thought. She turned her back on him as he prised open the lid of her cage.

'Come on, Mabel,' he said, but Mabel only turned even further away.

'Hurry up,' he said. 'We'll all be for it if Uncle Vince wakes up.'

'So you say,' said Mabel sulkily.

'Didn't you hear him?' said Frank. 'What did he say?'

'We heard what you wanted us to hear,' said Mabel, looking sly.

Frank was outraged.

'What did you say?' he said.

'Leave her, Frank,' called Elsie from below. 'There isn't time.'

In his armchair, Uncle Vince stirred. Frank hesitated, torn.

'He called me a real find,' Mabel went on dreamily. 'He said I had the most beautiful coat he'd ever seen.'

'Yes, but he wasn't going to leave it *on* you,' Frank said. 'He was going to take it for someone else.'

Mabel didn't respond to this, but looked cunning.

'Why should *I* follow *you*?' she said. 'That's what you've always wanted, isn't it, to rule over us all? Well, I'm not your lackey, you little squeaking rat. Go play follow-my-leader somewhere else.'

This was too much. Frank bared his yellow teeth. In a moment he would have leapt on Mabel from above and bitten her, but just then Uncle Vince shifted and mumbled, and there was a chorus of anxious squeaks from below.

'Come on, Frank!'

'Oh, do hurry up!'

'Leave her there if she doesn't want to come!'

'There isn't *time*!'

Frank made a decision. Terrible as it would be to leave Mabel, he could hardly let her endanger the others. He turned away and began to climb down.

'I've had enough of this,' he said over his shoulder. 'If you want to stay to be made into a pair of mittens or a baby's hat, it's up to you.'

But Mabel didn't really want to be left.

'Oh, all right, then,' she said in a superior tone. 'I suppose I'm not doing anything else.' And with a maddening slowness she climbed out of her cage and followed Frank all the way down to the carpet, making a dreadful fuss about the tenderness of her paws and the dust on the surfaces.

Maurice was speechless as she landed heavily next to him.

'Oh, my angel,' he gibbered. 'At last, at last!'

Mabel reared and cuffed him sharply.

'Out of my way, mouse-dropping,' she said, and pushed past him to the front of the little group. 'Well, go on, then,' she said to Frank. 'Lead on, if you know the way.'

Mabel was standing close enough to Frank for him to bite her, and he barely restrained himself, but this was not the time to make a scene. He pushed her out of the way, then led the little group across the carpet to the kitchen. He had decided that he would have to take them to the Room Beneath because there was no time to explore other avenues of escape. Unpleasant as that would be, it would at least convince them all that there really was something to be scared about.

Just as they were crossing the kitchen floor towards the door that led to the Room Beneath, Uncle Vince woke up.

First there was a rumbling snort.

Then a harsh and raucous cough.

Then a thump as the chair tilted backwards and landed again.

The hamsters froze where they were, one behind another on the tiles of the kitchen floor. Frank looked wildly around.

To the left there was a tall cupboard, and at the bottom where it joined the floor there was a gap.

In the front room the armchair creaked and groaned and Uncle Vince gave a huge noisy yawn. Little Drew whimpered in fear.

'Behind the cupboard, all of you,' Frank commanded. 'And don't move – not a whisker, not a squeak. Felicity, Drew, you first.'

Even as Frank spoke there was a creaking groan from the armchair as Uncle Vince stood up, followed by a moment of absolute silence. Then there was a tremendous, deafening, ear-blasting roar. All the hamsters flattened themselves to the floor and trembled in horror.

Frank was the first to recover. He seized Daisy, who happened to be nearest to him, and gave her a great shove into the gap behind the chipboard at the bottom of the cupboard.

'Hide, quickly, all of you!' he whispered, and he was about to bundle Felicity and Drew in after Daisy when Mabel pushed past them both, quickly followed by Maurice.

More roaring came from the lounge and there was the thud of approaching footsteps.

'It's hopeless,' Frank thought, as Chestnut squeezed himself slowly and painfully into the gap after Elsie. 'We'll all be caught.'

'Where are you, you little vermin?' Uncle Vince roared. They could hear him knocking the cages to the floor, then his footsteps pounded towards the kitchen.

Frank helped to push George into the crowded

space beneath the cupboard, then he started to push himself in, backwards, so that he could still peep out and see what was going on. There was much muffled groaning and squeaking as he stuffed himself in. George tugged Frank's pelt so hard to help him that it pinched.

Just in time!

The kitchen door slammed into the cupboard as Uncle Vince flung it open so violently that the handle made a dent in the side of it and the whole cupboard shook. He thundered around the kitchen, flinging cupboard doors open and throwing the contents out. There was a series of terrific crashes as pans and pan lids hit the tiles, and the sound of breaking glass.

Cramped in their rather dirty, smelly hiding place, the hamsters trembled and quaked, clutching one another in the darkness. Uncle Vince's great boots thudded right over to the cupboard beneath which they were all hiding.

'Right, you little rats!' he snarled, flinging the door open. 'Give yourselves up now, or I'll skin you alive instead of wringing your necks first!'

Frank closed his eyes. What if there was a hole in the floor of the cupboard through which Uncle Vince could see where they were all hiding? Frank knew from experience how many holes and cracks there were in cupboards. And what if one of the hamsters whimpered or squeaked? There would be nothing he could do. 'Courage!' he told himself quietly.

Suddenly Uncle Vince stopped rummaging around. He stood in front of the cupboard, saying nothing, breathing hard. Frank couldn't bear to look, and he couldn't bear not to. The silence was almost as horrible as the noise.

Cautiously he opened one eye, peeping out.

Uncle Vince was standing absolutely still in the middle of the kitchen floor. All around him there was a great ransacked heap of pots and pans and brushes and broken glass. He stood still, with his eyes closed and his head tilted upwards, almost as though he was sniffing.

Then, in a lightning movement, he turned to the door that led to the Room Beneath, and pulled it open. The horrifying odour of dead bodies flooded into the kitchen and Frank felt the hamsters behind him stiffen with shock. 'Now they can smell it,' he thought, and if the situation hadn't been so desperate he would have felt some satisfaction at being proved right.

Uncle Vince went through the door, his footsteps clattered down the stairs, then up again. Frank almost fell out of his hiding place attempting to see. Behind him the hamsters squirmed and moaned.

'Oh, what's happening?' they murmured, and 'I'm getting cramp!'

'Shhhh!' said Frank as Uncle Vince returned.

Then a great beam of light swept across the kitchen, over the ceilings and walls. Vince strode purposefully over to the sink on the far wall and began shining the torch into the spaces behind the cupboards!

Frank knew that unless he did something they were all lost.

But what could he do?

The door to the lounge was open and so, Frank realized, was the door to the Room Beneath.

Uncle Vince threw the back door open and shone the torch light round the yard at the rear of the house.

They would have to make a dash for it, now, while Uncle Vince's back was turned.

There was no time to lose.

'Follow me, everyone,' Frank said as urgently as possible in a whisper, and he set off right away towards the open door through which the stench of death was wafting.

It seemed like miles across the kitchen floor to the cellar door and, because he was leading the way, Frank couldn't really stop to check that they were all following. He had to hope that the hamsters would be more afraid of Uncle Vince by now than of the smell from the Room Beneath, and also that Uncle Vince would stay outside. Only when he reached the doorway did he pause to look over his shoulder. There, to his relief, were George and Chestnut, looking frightened and grim, and behind them he could make out the shadowy forms of Maurice and Elsie, the whiteness of Mabel. With a movement of his head he beckoned them, before dropping down the first step.

'What's that smell, Mummy?' Drew whimpered, but they all followed Frank down the stairs. Frank felt quite shaky with relief. He heard Uncle Vince return to the kitchen, then continue his search behind the cupboards. It sounded as though he was pulling them all apart. Frank went down the stairs slowly, one by one, to give everyone else the chance to follow.

Suddenly there was silence above. Frank's heart beat faster. They were nearly at the bottom of the stairs. Then behind them the door was kicked shut with a deafening crash, and Felicity squeaked. They were shut into the Room Beneath and Frank could only hope he could get them all out.

But not all the hamsters had reached the comparative safety of the Room Beneath. One small, grey-white hamster with a stumpy paw was still limping valiantly towards the door when Uncle Vince kicked it shut.

Yes, it was Daisy. She had been trapped right at the back of the space behind the cupboard. Mabel had followed her in and crushed her, leaning heavily on her hindquarters and her injured paw. All the time she had been in the cramped space Daisy had felt suffocated and in pain. By the time the other hamsters had left, she was feeling sick and dizzy, and she could hardly put her damaged paw down at all. But she was too brave to say anything or to draw attention to herself. She just limped after the others as fast as she could. When she heard Uncle Vince coming in from the backyard, she had almost stopped in terror, but then she had hobbled on gamely, trying not to hear his great footsteps as he approached, because in fact, on this particular bit of open floor, there was nowhere to hide.

Uncle Vince's huge black boots swerved so that they were right in front of Daisy. He pushed the door to the lounge shut before kicking closed the door to the Room Beneath. There was nowhere for Daisy to run. Uncle Vince reached down and with two great fingers picked Daisy up by the scruff of the neck. He held her in mid-air, inches from his face. Daisy kicked and squirmed in the long blast of sour, smelly breath.

'Gotcha,' said Uncle Vince.

6 Escape

There was a terrible noise when all the hamsters finally stood on the floor of the Room Beneath. There were moans and groans and lamentations. Elsie covered her eyes, George looked sick and Maurice fainted clean away. Felicity burst into tears and held Drew tightly against her so that he couldn't see, though he kept squeaking, 'What is it, Mum? I want to see, what is it?'

Chestnut kept staring around and shaking his head, repeating, 'I don't believe it,' and 'I never seen anything like it – not in all my days,' over and over again.

Mabel, for once, was speechless.

The shock temporarily distracted them. Even George was too busy trying to resuscitate Maurice to notice that Daisy was missing.

Frank didn't notice either. He left the rest to recover and got on with examining the room, pleased that he had explored it before and so at least he knew his way around all the boxes and tins and pipes. He had found out that it was possible to climb up the pipes and the ladder to a stack of tins next to the sink, and to run around the rim of the sink to the taps. Below the taps there was a hole, not the plug hole, but one which led to a pipe. He hadn't been very far along this pipe but he was certain it led to the outside world. This seemed to be the best way out of the little underground room, since the chink that led to the Spaces Between was too high up the wall. He searched for other gaps and crannies without success. It looked as though he would have to persuade them all to follow him into that hole in the sink.

Frank had never been down a hole in a sink before and wasn't sure where it might lead. He knew vaguely about pipes and sewers, because Guy had called plumbers in on several occasions. Once the water board had come to the house and had started drilling outside the backyard. Frank had watched with interest and had made Guy explain to him about sewers. So now he had a vague idea that all the houses' pipes joined up outside at the back, and it was possible to follow them beneath the streets of the town. In spite of the danger, he felt quite excited at the prospect of following the pipes, but he wasn't sure that the other hamsters would feel the same.

As he went on searching, a thought began to tremble at the back of Frank's mind – a thought that he hardly dared admit. It was a thought he'd had before, sometimes in his dreams, about starting his own tribe of hamsters in the Wild. He had put it to George and Elsie once, the very first time he'd met them, but they hadn't been interested. Now surely, though, they would see what a terrible thing it was to be Owned, dependent on the goodwill of the humans who looked after them. It was no life for a hamster. Hamsters belonged in the desert, where they could live wild and courageous and free. All the hamsters in captivity, everywhere in the world, had been bred from the original thirteen in the deserts of Syria. A mother and her twelve cubs. That was all it took. There were nine hamsters here, including Drew. They could make burrows, establish dens, flourish and multiply. All they had to do was to take the first step towards freedom. Surely now they would follow Frank into the Wild? He turned to the huddled group.

It was so dark Frank could hardly make them out, but he could just see that Elsie and George were busy trying to revive Maurice, Felicity had curled herself over Drew, who was sniffing quietly, and Chestnut was still in a daze, looking around and murmuring 'I don't believe it' to himself.

They didn't look too promising as a tribe, but Frank had to start somewhere. He cleared his throat.

'Fellow hamsters,' he began, and they all looked at him blankly. 'You are not free from danger yet. We have to leave this house. I can get you out. But before I do we have to consider where we want to go. Do you want to stay in captivity? Or should we try to make a new life for ourselves?'

'Oh, here we go,' said Mabel. 'Are you going to get us out of this – this *hole* or not?'

Frank licked his lips.

'I want you to think about what got you into this mess in the first place,' he said. 'Think about what it means to be at the mercy of humans –'

'You never give up, do you?' Mabel interrupted. 'You won't be happy until we're all living in the dirt and eating worms. Or the worms are eating *us*.'

Frank ignored her.

'Hamsters weren't meant to live in cages,' he went on. 'They were meant to live in tribes beneath the desert sands – to mate and multiply and grow strong. That's what we've been doing since the world began.'

Frank's voice grew stronger as his vision took hold, the vision of countless generations of hamsters living free.

'But – where's the desert from here, then?' asked Chestnut.

Frank paused. He knew he couldn't take them to the desert. He had only the vaguest idea where it was.

'It doesn't have to be the desert,' he said. 'It could be anywhere away from houses. Just across the street there's an open stretch of land – the Wild – where there's plenty of room to dig and burrow –'

The hamsters were looking at him in alarm.

'But who'd feed us?' they said.

Mabel gave a snort of laughter. 'You wouldn't have to worry about that for long,' she said. 'More like, who'd be feeding *on* you.'

Felicity wailed and covered her eyes.

'We would feed one another,' said Frank. 'And look out for one another as well. That's how hamsters flourish.'

Mabel took a step forward.

'The Wild?' she said. 'Isn't that where Mrs Timms's cats prowl at night, and owls hunt, and the little common fieldmice live out their short and squeaky lives? Where, in order to live, you have to hunt and kill?'

'Oh, take us back to the pet shop, please,' begged Felicity.

Maurice said faintly, 'I – don't – think – I – can – *take* – any – more – adventures.'

Chestnut said, 'I don't know about this Owner. I never seen anything like this – not *ever* – but Mr Wiggs was always good to us. I miss Old Wiggsy.'

'I miss Lucy,' Elsie said.

'It's not that we don't appreciate what you've done for us,' Chestnut went on. 'But it seems to me, begging your pardon, that you want to lead us from one mortal danger to another. And us, well, we just want to live peaceful lives. And we've all got homes to go to. So, if you could do us another great kindness and take us back, well, we'd all be deeply obliged. In fact, *obliged* isn't the right word, nor grateful neither. Well, we'd owe you a huge debt, young buck. We'd take our hats off to you – if we had any, that is.'

Chestnut peered at Frank earnestly in the gloom. Frank stared back at the little cluster of hamsters. They all looked scared and rather sorry for themselves, except for Mabel, who just looked scornful. George hung on to Maurice, who had begun to revive and was moaning 'Oh, my head,' and 'Is it all over yet?' in a pitiful way. Elsie, like Felicity, was cowering over Drew.

They really didn't look much like a tribe. As Frank looked at them all, his arguments faded away. 'But I have to take them somewhere,' he thought. It wasn't safe to stay here. Maybe later, when they'd all realized they could survive out of their cages, he could try again. Reluctantly, he let go of his vision.

'Is that what you want – to go back to the pet shop?' he said.

Mabel replied, 'Of course it is. They don't want to be owl fodder. They might as well stay here. Are you going to take us home or not?'

Frank scowled at Mabel, ready to say many sharp things, but at that moment they all heard Uncle Vince's footsteps again, approaching the top of the stairs.

There wasn't a moment to lose.

'Quick, follow me,' Frank hissed, and he ran along a plank of wood and up the side of a large box, finding footings easily in the ridges in the cardboard.

Above them Uncle Vince's footsteps retreated, then returned, then went away again.

The box took Frank to a narrow pipe that ran along the back wall. He followed it until his progress was blocked by a wooden ladder. This, however, was old, with many cracks and chips in it, and therefore relatively easy for a hamster to scale. Frank climbed up the side of it a little way and then dropped on to a rung. From here he could reach the stack of tins next to the sink. The tins were covered in globules and crusty frills of dried paint which helped him to reach the lid of the top one. This was almost level with the sink and, by stretching and kicking, Frank hauled himself over the rim of the sink.

He clung to the rim for a moment, checking that

the other hamsters were following. There they all were, struggling a bit and grumbling. George was helping Chestnut and Maurice, Elsie was helping Felicity with Drew, and Mabel, as far as he could see, was pushing all the others out of the way. Frank dropped into the sink and waited for the rest to join him, which, after much slipping about and complaining, they did.

'Ugh, it's wet,' said Mabel.

'And cold,' said Felicity.

'I've got paint on my paws,' said Elsie.

'I think I've got splinters,' said Maurice.

'Frank –' said George, a little breathlessly.

'Not now, George,' said Frank. 'There isn't time. Listen, all of you. This is our escape route. At the back of this opening here,' he reached up and touched it, 'there's a pipe leading out of the house. It connects to other pipes which we can follow. Don't ask me where, because I don't know. But the point is: it's a way out – a way to freedom.'

'But Frank–' George began before his voice was drowned in a clamour of protest.

'Down there? I can't!'

'Surely not.'

'You can't be serious. It's *filthy*!'

'I told you the little pip-squeak would lead you straight into the mire!'

'Frank, *listen*!' George tried again.

But Chestnut interrupted him, 'I think *we're* the ones who should listen – to Frank. Now I'm not any more keen than you to climb into that murky hole, but if Frank says it's the only way then I'm prepared to try, and so should you be. After all, he's got us all this far. We're all here at least and –'

'But that's just the *point*!' George burst in. He was hopping up and down excitedly. 'We're not all here! Daisy isn't here. Where's Daisy?'

There was a stunned silence. Then all the hamsters began talking at once.

'I thought she was with you.'

'She was just behind Mabel.'

'Did you see her?'

'No, I didn't see her. I thought you saw her.'

'All right, all right. Who was the last to see her?'

Silence.

Frank felt terrible. He was the leader and he should have checked. Why hadn't he noticed that she wasn't with them?

Elsie said slowly, 'She was with us behind the cupboard.'

Chestnut said, 'But did she make it to the stairs?'

No one said anything to this.

Then Mabel said, snappily, 'Well, we can't wait around here much longer. If she didn't make it, tough. We have to get going.'

George drew himself up. 'I'm not going anywhere without Daisy,' he said.

'George, you *have* to,' said Elsie, but Frank could tell that George meant it. Frank thought hard, but he couldn't think what to do. Eight pairs of eyes were fastened on him, waiting for him to speak. Finally he cleared his throat.

'Well,' he said.

But just at that moment the latch to the cellar door clicked and the door opened!

'Quick, all of you!' said Frank. Knowing that he would have to lead the way, he hoisted himself into the grimy hole.

Chestnut and Elsie shoved George up after Frank, though he kicked and struggled. Next they started to help Felicity and Drew, but Maurice scrambled past them quickly and clambered in. Then Mabel, thrusting them aside, heaved herself in with a snort of disgust. She was so fat she got stuck and had to be pushed from behind. Next Felicity held Drew up and he clambered from her shoulders into the hole. Hastily she thrust herself in after him, climbing on Chestnut's shoulders to reach the hole.

Above them the light was switched on. A bald bulb flared down at them from the middle of the ceiling. Elsie and Chestnut cowered, dazzled, as Uncle Vince's footsteps thudded heavily down the stairs.

'After you,' Chestnut said, panting a little from his exertions, and he gave Elsie a paw up into the hole.

Just as she was squeezing in, Elsie heard an ear-splitting yell from behind.

Uncle Vince had seen them!

Elsie kicked furiously and slid round a long bend in the pipe. She could just hear Chestnut sliding in after her, but there was hardly time to feel relieved, because this pipe joined another, and just below the junction there was a cold, slimy pool. Unable to stop herself, she slid straight into the water with a soft plop. Her nose, eyes, ears and mouth quickly filled with mucky water so she couldn't see or breathe.

Hamsters aren't used to swimming, being desert creatures. It was horrible. The water had bits floating in it – Elsie hardly dared think what they were – and long strands of what felt like hair. Worse, the pipe curved downwards and then steeply up. Elsie squirmed and struggled, but she couldn't break through to the surface of the water. She struggled upwards, sank down again, pushed back against Chestnut, rose towards the surface, but sank once more.

Behind her Chestnut kicked heroically, but he couldn't push Elsie's weight up as well as his own. They were both trapped in the watery bend.

Beneath Elsie's panic there was a calm feeling similar to despair. 'It's all right now,' a voice said in her mind. 'Everything's all right.' She stopped struggling and closed her eyes, feeling strangely peaceful.

The next moment there was a terrific pumping and sucking sensation and the water around Elsie and

Chestnut began to swirl and churn. They were moving! Up over the next bend in the pipe, then down, down, choking and spluttering as their noses broke the surface of the water. As they surfaced they could hear Uncle Vince's angry cries and the PUMP PUMP PUMP of what sounded like a huge machine that was making the whole pipe shake.

Unwittingly, Uncle Vince was helping them. He had attacked the plug hole with a huge plunger, thinking that he would suck the hamsters back along the pipe. Most fortunately for them, he only managed to disturb the water in the U-bend and force it forward. It gushed along the pipe, carrying Elsie and Chestnut with it.

When the pipe levelled out, they were able to run through the shallow water and soon heard Frank's voice calling them from up ahead.

'This way! This way!' he encouraged them.

The water receded to a thin trickle and Frank scurried along the pipe to meet them. Still coughing and spluttering, they followed him into a kind of chamber, with pipes and tunnels leading off it. Here Elsie sank down, shivering uncontrollably.

All the hamsters were there. They looked wretched – sick and grimy and soaked. Drew was whimpering as Felicity tried feebly to lick him clean. Maurice lay on his back with his paws in the air. Mabel was grooming herself vigorously in disgust. Only George was on his feet, looking shaken, but determined.

Frank looked worse than any of them. He had

gone through the pool first. He had taken with him most of the smelly muck with which it had become blocked through years of disuse. He was covered in matted hair, grease and what looked like bits of old food that he tried in vain to scrape off. Eventually he gave up and stood in the middle of the little chamber, looking around at the bedraggled group of hamsters.

'Well,' he said finally, 'we've made it, anyway. We're safe.'

'*Safe!*' snorted Mabel furiously. 'I'm glad you call being half drowned and *slimed* to death safe.'

Frank ignored her.

'The question is,' he said, 'where are we going from here?'

'You mean you don't know?' said Mabel. 'What kind of a leader are you?'

Frank ran round the little chamber, sniffing at all the different exits. One was larger than the others and sloped downwards. A greater variety of evil scents wafted towards him from this musty opening than from the others.

'This must be the pipe that leads to the main sewer,' he said, hoping that he sounded more confident than he felt. 'We could follow this and see where it takes us.'

'*See where it takes us!*' squawked Mabel. 'Do you mean to say that after dragging us here – nearly killing us in the process – *you don't know the way*?'

Frank was about to answer when there was a horrible gurgling rush from the pipe behind them. All the hamsters squeaked in terror as water spurted into the chamber from the pipe they had just left. Mabel ran into one of the other pipes. Felicity grabbed Drew and hoisted him on to her back. Meanwhile Maurice scrambled to his feet and attempted to climb the side of the chamber.

It was Uncle Vince again. He realized that the hamsters had all disappeared along the pipe behind the sink. When he couldn't get them back, he had rammed the plug into the plug hole and turned both taps on. As the sink filled, water began to flow out of the opening through which the hamsters had escaped (which was there for that very purpose, in fact, to prevent the sink from overflowing). Once he judged that enough water had gone down the overflow to drown any hamster still lodged there, he released the plug and let the whole sinkful of water gush down the plug hole to the pipe beneath, which led straight to the little chamber.

All the hamsters clung to the sides of the chamber as the water churned towards them in a great wave. Elsie closed her eyes. 'We are all lost,' she thought, sadly. 'Now, after coming so far.'

However, instead of flooding the little chamber, the water emptied out of the largest hole, which, as Frank had detected, led downwards.

The hamsters stared at the water blankly as it drained away, then let out a collective sigh of relief.

'That was a close shave,' said Chestnut.

'My nerves won't stand much more of this,' said Maurice.

'*Please* take us home,' Felicity begged.

'Home?' said Mabel, coming out of her pipe. 'Didn't you hear Frank? He doesn't know where home is.'

In fact Frank now knew that the large hole at the back did lead to the main sewer. This was the pipe they would have to follow in order to return to the pet shop. The other pipes, which were smaller and pointed upwards, must lead into the other houses on Bright Street.

Hardly had he come to this conclusion when there was another gurgle from the pipe where Mabel had sheltered, and all the hamsters squeaked in alarm again.

'Stand back, all of you,' Frank ordered. 'Don't panic!'

The hamsters, somewhat squeakily, did as they were told. This time the water only gushed over their paws before trickling away through the large opening at the back.

This confirmed everything that Frank had just been thinking. He told the other hamsters what he now knew.

'This pipe leads to the main sewer, to the outside,' he said, walking over to the large opening. 'All the others go into houses. So it depends where you want to go from here.'

'I'm going back,' said George.

Mabel snorted. 'You're welcome!' she said. 'Just point me in the direction of home and I'll be off, thank you very much.'

'We want to go back to the pet shop,' said Felicity.

Chestnut agreed.

Maurice gave a pathetic croak of assent.

Elsie found her voice. 'George dear, you can't go *back*. Not to that terrible place. We barely survived getting here.'

George looked fearful but stubborn.

'I can't just leave her, Elsie,' he said, and Elsie could tell that he meant it.

Frank licked his lips. This was a real predicament. He blamed himself for Daisy being left behind. He should have noticed sooner. The others had all been too overwhelmed by the horrors of the Room Beneath to realize that Daisy wasn't with them, but he should have checked. Now it would be nearly impossible to get back through the pipes. He couldn't put them all through it again. Nevertheless, he couldn't let George return on his own.

'What are we all waiting for?' Mabel asked. 'Just tell me how to get home!'

'We want to get home too,' said Felicity.

Chestnut said, 'We all want to get home, and Frank'll tell us how. He's just thinking, aren't you, Frank?'

Frank *was* thinking. He was thinking that he didn't know which tunnel led to which house. He didn't know how Mabel could get back to number 11 Bright Street. Nor did he really know how to get the rest of them back to the pet shop. All he knew was that it should be possible to follow the main sewer under the streets to Mr Wiggs' shop and that one of the smaller pipes should take Mabel home. But which one? He began to walk round the chamber slowly, sniffing at all the different exits. Behind him Maurice struggled to his feet.

'My paws hurt,' he moaned.

'Don't you worry, son,' Chestnut said. 'Frank knows what he's doing.'

'If only that were true,' Frank thought, aware that they were all watching him. He sniffed all the exits very thoroughly, partly to buy himself some more time. They all smelled equally bad.

Behind him Mabel stomped about impatiently.

'Well come *on*!' she exclaimed. 'I haven't got all day.'

Frank turned round.

'I think it's this one,' he said.

'You *think*?' said Mabel. 'You mean you still don't *know*?'

'No, I don't know,' Frank snapped. 'I'm trying to work it out. Just like you should be doing. Instead of just sitting there waiting for it all to be done for you.'

Mabel drew herself up.

'I'm not the one who got us into this mess,' she hissed. 'You're good at getting us into messes, aren't you? Well, now it's time to get us out of one.'

It was Frank's turn to draw himself up.

'If you think you can do any better –' he began.

'Stop it, both of you,' Elsie said. 'This isn't getting us anywhere. We've got to sort this out. We all want to go different ways. Mabel wants to go home and so do I. The rest of you want to go back to the pet shop. And George – George?'

Elsie looked wildly around the little chamber.

'Where's George?' she cried.

There was a pause, then Maurice said, 'He went back up that tunnel a few moments ago.'

'And you didn't try to stop him?' Elsie wailed.

'*Me* stop him?' gasped Maurice in astonishment. 'You all heard what he said about going back for Daisy. I thought you all knew he'd gone.'

'We *have* to stop him!' Elsie yelled, and she ran towards the tunnel that led back to the sink.

'Elsie, wait, please!' cried Frank.

Then Mabel said, 'Oh, let her go for goodness' sake. If they're so keen on getting themselves killed, let them get on with it. Now, let's get going.'

Elsie rounded on Mabel. 'This is all your fault!' she cried.

'*My* fault?' said Mabel. 'Whatever do you mean?'

'You were the one who wanted to stay in that house! If you hadn't taken so long to come with us, we'd have got away sooner – and we wouldn't have left Daisy behind!'

Elsie was almost in tears, partly because of worrying about George and partly at the prospect of going after him and tackling the flooded pipes again. Mabel looked furious, as if she might attack her.

Frank said, 'Stop it, both of you, *right now*.'

There was a complete silence that stretched out like a rubber band. Frank had no idea what he was going to say next, but he had to say something. Finally he spoke.

'I think we should all stay together. The group's

falling apart. Elsie, it's too dangerous to go back after George. Mabel, I don't know which of these pipes will go back to your house. But I do know that the large opening will take us to the main sewer. And from there we might – we just might – find our way to Mr Wiggs' pet shop. Now, are you coming with me or not?'

'*No!*' said Elsie and Mabel together.

Mabel said, 'I'm not trekking through filthy pipes for miles when I'm this close to home. No way!'

Elsie said, 'It's no use, Frank, I can't leave George.'

Chestnut said, 'I wish someone would make their mind up.'

Frank felt as though his mind was being pulled in all directions. He didn't know what to do. He could see that both Elsie and Mabel were equally determined, but he didn't want to take the others back into danger or get them lost. He had so many conflicting thoughts he felt as though his head might burst. He closed his eyes to concentrate.

'What should I do?' he thought.

He had no idea who he was asking, or any real hope of an answer. Suddenly, part of his brain seemed to clear. And in it, something spoke into his thoughts.

'If you want hamsters to be free,' it said, 'treat them as though they were free.'

Frank opened his eyes. Elsie looked stubborn and Mabel looked fierce. He knew that he couldn't stop them from breaking away, and that trying to do so was a waste of time. However much he wanted to rescue George and Daisy, his job was to lead the rest of the hamsters to safety. He cleared his throat and, looking at Mabel and Elsie, he said: 'You're free, both of you, to decide which way you want to go. I'm going to the main sewer. I would prefer you to come with me, but that's up to you. I can't wait any longer.' He looked from one to the other. 'Elsie?'

Elsie seemed calmer now. Slowly she shook her head.

'I've got to try to find George,' she said.

'Mabel?' Frank said.

'No way,' Mabel said promptly. 'I want to go home, and I want to go home *now*.'

'Then, you're both on your own,' Frank said.

Elsie looked a little scared but she didn't say anything.

Mabel said, 'So, that's it? We're on our own while you lot all troop off together to save your own skins? Well, that's just fine. That's –'

'*Mabel!*' Frank interrupted sharply. 'No one's been more keen on saving her own skin than you. You've been selfish right from the start. You've held everyone up and you're doing it again now. Well, we're not going to be held up any longer. You've taken your decision. Maurice, Chestnut, Felicity, are you ready to follow me?'

Without a word the three hamsters and baby Drew got into a line behind Frank. Maurice followed Felicity and Chestnut brought up the rear. Elsie watched them with a lonely feeling clutching at her heart, then she turned to re-enter the tunnel that would take her to Uncle Vince's house, shuddering delicately as she followed the wet pipe. Mabel watched them all as if she couldn't quite believe what was happening. All along she had thought that if she really insisted they would have taken her home first.

'You're not actually going?' she said.

Maurice wouldn't look at her.

Mabel's voice rose shrilly. 'You're all mad,' she cried. 'I hope you all get lost – and – and – *drown*! Aren't you even going to tell me which tunnel to try, Frank?'

Frank looked over his shoulder.

'I'd try that one if I were you,' he said, nodding towards an opening that was in the middle of all the others. Mabel hurried over to it.

'This one?' she said. 'Why this one, Frank? Why?'

Frank had already entered the largest pipe.

'I don't know,' he called back, his voice echoing strangely. 'It seems as good as any. Why don't you go and find out for yourself? Because, just for once, Mabel, no one's going to do it for you.'

Mabel peered after their receding shapes, feeling furious and scared and lonely. If only Frank would come back so that she could bite him! But there was nothing she could do to make him return.

'I hope you all drown!' she shouted, and her voice echoed eerily along the pipe.

The echoes followed Frank as he pattered over the grit and shale scattered along the pipe, together with other, slimy, slippery remains. Rumbling and gurgling noises came from neighbouring pipes. From time to time, as they trotted on, there were holes in the wall of the pipe from which other pipes branched off. Frank trekked on doggedly, hoping against hope that he was following the right pipe.

Something told him that he was – something that he could only see when he wasn't looking directly at it. It was like a small, flickering column of flame, weaving ahead of him in the distance, and vanishing when he looked up. It was as though he could only see it in the same way as he had seen his vision of hamsters earlier, not in the same way as he saw the pipe and the hamsters following him now.

Whatever it was, he was glad of it, since the pipe was spooky and uncomfortable – wet and cold. It was all too easy to imagine being lost in it forever. Indeed, occasionally he came upon what looked like animal remains. These he always pushed aside, out of the path of the other hamsters, who were weary and dispirited enough, he could tell, from the occasional whimper and snivel behind. Whenever he spoke to them he tried to sound confident. In fact, he had never travelled so far underground as this, beneath what he judged must now be the streets of the town.

Frank had vague memories of the pet shop and Mr Wiggs, though he had been taken from there by Guy when only a tiny cub. Even so, hamsters never forget a direction. As always when underground, Frank's instincts were returning. He could remember that the pet shop was on a big street where there were other shops and a good deal of traffic. He *thought* that the big street was only two or three streets away from Guy's house. 'How long would it take to travel that far?' he wondered. He didn't get to finish the thought, because the next moment he slid on something wet and disgusting. His feet flew from under him and he skidded several inches along the pipe. Behind him, Felicity and Maurice cried out in alarm.

Frank picked himself up painfully, aware that the gurgling noises from the branching pipes seemed louder now. He raised his voice to make himself heard.

'It's all right,' he called. 'It's just a bit slippy. You have to be care–'

But Frank never got the chance to finish his sentence. Because just at that moment there was a roaring *whoosh* and, from the pipe they had just passed, a huge wave of water gushed.

It poured out of the pipe at such a tremendous rate that the stricken hamsters had no chance to escape. Before any of them could so much as squeak, the foaming flood had engulfed them all.

7 George to the Rescue

Up and up George climbed. It seemed further than he remembered, and much slippier since Uncle Vince had allowed water to overflow into the pipe. Hamsters are used to travelling up and down narrow tunnels. These tunnels are usually dry, unlike the pipe George was in. He climbed up and slid down, climbed up and slid down. At last he came to the drop which led directly to the U-bend that was full of water. Taking a deep breath, he plunged in, squirming and kicking. This time he was prepared. He writhed round at the point where the pipe curved steeply upwards and, with a final kick, his nose broke the surface of the water.

Barely an inch or two above this, a pipe branched off the main one and George knew that he had to go along it. The main one would take him straight to the plug hole, which would be much harder to get through into the sink. It was the branch pipe, curving into a kind of 'p' shape, which would take him to the overflow's opening .

As George scurried along this pipe he began to see light – a little yellow spot at the end of the pipe. He could hear a muffled voice as well, and smell sickly chemical fumes. His heart beat fast. What was happening to Daisy? With a final squirm and a struggle he emerged through the overflow into bright light.

Temporarily dazzled, George could only smell Uncle Vince (who still reeked of leather and cigarettes) and hear him.

'Come on now, my beauty, come to Uncle Vince. Mustn't be shy. Oh no. There we are. No biting, now. Ooops! It's a good job Uncle Vince has got his gloves on.'

George tried hard to make sense of the blurred shapes in the room. He could tell that Vince was in front of him, a big black shape with his back to the sink. He was between George and the table. There was some large covered object on the table, and behind it George could make out Daisy's cage. There were other objects on the table too and, as his eyes focused, he could make out a bottle from which the sickly smell seemed to be emanating, some swabs of cotton wool, and a small board.

Uncle Vince poured some liquid from the bottle on to a cotton-wool swab. At once the smell became powerful, still sickening, yet strangely familiar. It dulled the senses, making it difficult to think.

'This should calm you down,' Uncle Vince muttered. 'If you won't come out when I ask you nicely.' He pushed the swab of cotton wool into Daisy's cage.

Moments later he lifted Daisy out by the scruff of her neck. George watched, horrified, as she hung limply from Uncle Vince's fingers, without so much as a kick. Then Uncle Vince laid her out on the little board and bent over her for some time. George couldn't see what he was doing, and he trembled in rage and fear. When Uncle Vince finally straightened again and moved aside, George saw a sight so terrible that he had to clutch at the rim of the overflow's opening to stop himself falling back down the pipe.

Daisy was spreadeagled – stretched out on her back, her paws, including the little twisted stump, tied to four pegs at the corners of the board.

Oh, how George wanted to bite Uncle Vince! He wanted to sink his teeth into the thickly folded flesh of Uncle Vince's neck, and claw his face, but what could he do? All he could do was to stay where he was and hang on, choking back a wave of sickness, as Uncle Vince began to uncover the large bulging object on the table.

As the last plastic sheet was pulled away, George stared, trying to make sense of the bright metallic machinery. When he realized what it was he thought he might faint clean away.

It was a machine for making hamster skins out of hamsters. There were wheels and blades and scrapers, cutters and rollers and stretchers and containers full of chemicals for cleaning and treating the skins. Beneath it all there was a conveyor belt on to which Uncle Vince was placing Daisy on her board.

Furious with fear, George leapt out of the overflow and ran along the rim of the sink. He didn't know what he was going to do, but he had to do something. He had to rescue Daisy. But how was he going to get from the sink to the table?

As Uncle Vince moved along the monstrous machine, checking a part here and a liquid level there, George stared desperately around the room. Though close, the table was just too far away for him to jump, otherwise he would have risked it. It might be possible to climb the rough plaster to the shelf along the wall above the table, and to drop on to the table from it. However, that would surely attract Uncle Vince's attention.

George had never felt so helpless in all his life, not even in the hands of Jake and Josh. He was trying to think clearly, while all the time a voice in his head was shouting, 'Hurry! Hurry!' He wished with all his heart that Frank was there. What would Frank do? He always found a way.

Despairing, not even thinking of hiding, George stared around the room. He tried not to notice the hamster skins hanging on the line like a row of little, tragic flags, or to look at the terrible machine. Just then Uncle Vince's foot caught something that made the whole contraption rattle.

'Ooops,' he said, steadying it.

George stared. Leading down from the machine and across the floor there was a thick cable ending in a plug. Of course! If he could reach the cable he could climb on to the table and rescue Daisy. All he had to do was to get from the sink to the floor.

Trembling with nervous excitement, George ran along the rim of the sink and started to descend the same way they had first climbed up to it with Frank.

First, he jumped on to the top of the stack of paint

tins. He hoped fervently that they wouldn't rattle and that Vince wouldn't notice him. Then he stretched from the tins to the ladder and scrabbled quickly down its frame. He didn't even need the box this time because the ladder took him all the way to the floor. Now he ran along behind the box and emerged near the cable.

The cable was covered in a material that made it quite easy to climb, like a very thick rope. George's mind went blank at the thought of what he might do at the top, or what would happen if Uncle Vince spotted him. All he knew was that he had to get to Daisy.

Fortunately for George, Uncle Vince was so busy checking the wheels and cogs and rollers and cutting things that he didn't notice the nose and whiskers of a small, determined hamster appearing over the edge of the table. George set paw on the wooden surface just in time to see Uncle Vince pull down a lever on one side of the monstrous machine. The wheels whirred, the gears clicked, a piston pumped, and the whole thing swung smoothly and terribly into motion, the bright blades gleaming as they descended in a perfect arc.

George was horribly frightened. He had never been so close to machinery of any kind before, let alone to machinery of sinister and murderous intent. He was close enough to see exactly how it worked. The rollers rolled, the stretchers stretched, and little pincers for the hamster skins dunked them into small vats of fluid that would remove all traces of blood.

Then Daisy's skin would be pegged out on the line with all the others.

Not if George could help it! Overcoming his fear, he scurried along the side of the machine furthest away from Uncle Vince. He tried not to look at the gleaming, deadly parts as they churned and rolled and hummed in motion. Ahead he could see Daisy, still spreadeagled on the little board, moving on the conveyor belt towards the first blade. George would have to gnaw through the ties that bound her, rouse her, and get her away from the murderous machine before the cutting started – all right under Uncle Vince's nose! George's courage quailed at the thought of it and he stopped suddenly.

'I can't do it,' he thought.

Then, as if in answer to a prayer, the machinery halted. Uncle Vince had pulled down the lever again, and he was peering critically along the middle section.

'You need a drop of oil, my beauty,' he murmured. 'And a touch more cleaning fluid.' He turned away from the table!

There was no time to think. George ran to Daisy's board and began tugging at the little cords that were wound tightly round her paws and the four pegs. They were tougher than he'd thought, covered in some kind of waxy substance that made them hard to snap. George fumbled and tugged, sweating in fear as Uncle Vince's footsteps thudded around the room. The lid to the cleaning fluid came off with a metallic clatter, and more noxious fumes filled the air. George gripped one of the cords in his teeth, then pulled back with all his weight, terrified that he might hurt one of Daisy's good paws.

The cord snapped! As Vince applied oil to the wheels at the far end of the machine, George worked furiously on another cord. It snapped too. Quickly, he ran to another cord and snapped it, almost leaping out of his skin when Uncle Vince noisily cleared his throat.

The final cord proved the trickiest. George had to wind it through his teeth to get a proper grip. He leaned back as far as he could to stretch it fully, but it refused to snap. Daisy moaned a little and rolled over. George closed his eyes. Uncle Vince straightened.

Without warning, his footsteps clattered towards them.

'What have we got here?' he said, in his rasping voice. George cowered, his eyes still shut. 'It's all over now,' he thought, and he waited for Uncle Vince's hand to descend.

But it didn't.

'All right, sweetheart,' Uncle Vince murmured. 'Just – stay – exactly – where – you – are.'

It didn't sound as if he was talking to George. Fearfully, George opened one eye.

Uncle Vince was walking towards the sink. He had picked up a plant pot from the nearby shelf and was holding it upside-down in his hand.

And standing before him on the rim of the sink was Elsie.

She had struggled along the pipe after George, plunging, terrified, into the murky water trapped in the U-bend and this time managing to kick her way out. She had climbed up the narrow tube of the overflow just minutes after George, and she had witnessed everything from the hole at the back of the sink. She had seen Uncle Vince set the monstrous machinery in motion. She had seen Daisy, bound and helpless, put into it. She had watched, heart in mouth, as George climbed on to the table, inches away from Uncle Vince. She had barely stopped herself squeaking aloud when Uncle Vince had turned away and George had immediately run to Daisy and started tugging at the cords. She felt faint and dizzy with anxiety as Uncle Vince searched for oil along the row of tins on the shelf. When he had found it, she knew he would turn back to the machinery and see George.

Uncle Vince had turned, but he didn't see George. He started to oil the end of the machine furthest from George. Elsie swallowed the sickness she felt as he moved further along the machine, oiling the tiny cogs and gears. Any moment now he would look along the length of it and see George. Elsie knew what she had to do. As Uncle Vince straightened, she climbed out of the overflow and shot along the rim of the sink, hoping to distract him from George.

It was working. Uncle Vince came slowly towards Elsie, watching her all the time.

George was terrified, but he knew he had to make the most of this chance. Hastily he snapped the final cord. As Daisy moaned and stirred, he began to tug her back into her cage. His only hope was to hide her there, where Uncle Vince wouldn't think of looking, until she recovered enough to follow him. Uncle Vince wouldn't think of looking in her cage when he'd discovered she'd escaped. He tugged her in through the cage's open door and began burrowing furiously into the wood-shavings.

Meanwhile, Elsie slowly edged away from Uncle Vince.

'Come on, my poppet, my princess,' he crooned. 'Come to Uncle Vince. There now, there now, shhh.'

He raised the plant pot, ready to bring it down over Elsie.

Elsie moved away from Uncle Vince in the opposite direction from the ladder and the stack of tins. To her right was the shelf with the tins on. It seemed impossibly far away, but there was a rag dangling from the end nearest her. As Uncle Vince stepped up to her, Elsie knew she would have to resort to her ultimate tactic – the Lightning Twist Propulsion Manoeuvre she had once taught George. This involved contracting all her muscles at once, then releasing them like a spring.

Elsie leapt towards the shelf.

She flew through the air with her paws outstretched – and just caught the bottom edge of the rag. Very fortunately for Elsie, it didn't come away from the shelf as she clutched it. Its other end was trapped under a heavy tin. She swung perilously for a moment as Uncle Vince's great fingers snatched at her. Then, by contracting all her muscles again, she propelled herself upwards along the rag and hoisted herself on to the shelf. Once there, she ran as fast as she could behind all the tins and pots, but Uncle Vince's hand came after her, sweeping them all to the floor.

How George trembled for Elsie as the tremendous clatter went on. He carried on chafing Daisy's paws and patting her cheek pouches in an attempt to rouse her, but even the terrible noise did little more than make her moan.

'Don't leave me,' she whimpered, her head lolling against his pelt.

'I'll never leave you again,' George whispered. 'Daisy, wake up, *please.*'

But Daisy only lapsed back into unconsciousness.

In a fit of anxiety, George ran to the door of the cage. He craned his head out in time to see Elsie reach the end of the shelf and pause, while behind her Uncle Vince swept the final pots to the floor.

'*Elsie,*' George squeaked. He had to do something and he had to do it now.

I don't know if you've ever seen how fast a

hamster can dart, but it really is extraordinary. George darted now, beneath the blades and teeth of the monstrous machine to the little lever on the other side that Uncle Vince had used before. He ran up the gears and pulleys and dropped on to it with all his weight.

It worked. The gears ground, the wheels rattled and the pulleys swung into motion. Uncle Vince lurched round so fast that he almost fell over. George barely had time to dash back into the cage before he lunged at the deathly machine.

'What's going on?' he bellowed.

Of course, this gave Elsie time to descend from the shelf, using the end of the line on which all the hamster skins were pegged out. The line dangled into a woven bag full of pegs that stood on a box. Shuddering because she was so close to the sad little skins, Elsie dropped into the peg bag and hid.

And all Uncle Vince saw as he switched off his ghastly machine was the empty board with its four tattered cords, and a space on the shelf where Elsie should have been.

Uncle Vince's fury was horrible to hear. Roaring, he swept the empty board off the conveyor belt. Next, he seized Daisy's cage, shook it violently, and threw it with all his strength at the wall. The cage burst apart and wood-shavings spilled everywhere. George and Daisy were winded by the fall, but fortunately the wood-shavings protected them. The cage landed in such a way that they were still mostly hidden. Uncle Vince, in any case, wasn't looking for them. He swept the pots and tins off the shelf with a terrific clatter as they cowered in the wood-shavings. They heard him thunder up the stairs, still roaring, and slam the door so hard it almost fell off its hinges.

The silence that followed was deafening. Elsie peeped out of the peg bag.

'George! George!' she called. 'Are you all right, George?'

There was a cough and a shuffle, and the tip of George's nose appeared from a pile of wood-shavings.

'Over here,' he said weakly.

Elsie scurried over to him.

'Oh George, are you hurt?'

George squirmed out from beneath the mangled cage.

'I'm all right, I think,' he said slowly. 'But Elsie, you were wonderful!'

'I was so scared when I saw Uncle Vince and that – that horrible machine!'

'Me too. And Daisy was all tied up ...'

'... And you were untying her, right under his nose ...'

'... But I couldn't get the cord undone ...'

'... But you didn't run away. Oh George, you were wonderful too.'

And they went on like this for several moments while Elsie cleaned the wood-shavings out of George's ears and groomed him just as she used to. A vivid memory returned to them of how they had both escaped from danger once before by fooling a cat. Elsie had hidden George in her cage, just as he had hidden Daisy. Elsie was so proud of George, and he of her, that they just looked at one another with shining eyes.

There was a moan and a scuffling noise, and Daisy's face appeared from under what was left of the wheel.

'Wha'sh time?' she mumbled in a slurred voice. 'Where'sh party?' And she sank down in the wood-shavings.

George and Elsie hurried over to her. They each took a paw to help Daisy, but Daisy was still not moving too well and she was still very much inclined to fall asleep.

'Daisy,' called Elsie. 'Daisy, dear!' She felt almost kindly disposed towards Daisy since she had helped to save her life.

'I'll help her,' said George, as Daisy merely mumbled and snorted. He got behind her and pushed, while Elsie, who was getting anxious now in case Uncle Vince returned, tugged at the front end until Daisy emerged fully, looking very groggy and covered in wood-shavings.

'Back to sleep,' she said, sinking down.

George and Elsie looked at one another. They still had to get her to the sink.

'Come on, Daisy,' George said, tapping her cheek pouches. 'Wake up now, we've got to go.'

Daisy opened one eye.

'I feel sick,' she said, and closed it again.

'Here, let me have a go,' said Elsie. She stepped forward and smacked poor Daisy smartly on the nose. 'Get up,' she said.

'*Owww!*' said Daisy, but she opened both eyes this time. 'That hurt!'

'You will be hurt if Uncle Vince comes back,' said Elsie.

As if on cue they heard footsteps upstairs.

All three hamsters froze. George was the first to recover.

'Quick!' he said commandingly. 'The ladder!'

Between them they hauled Daisy over to the plank which led to the box of ridged cardboard, which led in turn to the ladder. Elsie led the way and George followed Daisy to make sure she didn't slip. One by one they scaled the ladder to the tins of paint. From there they climbed over the rim of the sink, only too aware all the time of Uncle Vince's heavy tread.

'Wh-where are we going?' Daisy gasped. Fear had brought her round quickly and made her alert.

'We have to go through this hole, here,' George explained. 'There's a pipe, and you come to some water and you have to kick – hard.'

'Down there? I can't,' said Daisy, panicking, but Elsie gave her a little push.

'You're a hamster, aren't you?' she said sternly. 'Get tunnelling.'

For a moment it looked as though Daisy might argue. Then there was the ominous click of the cellar door. With a squeak of alarm, Daisy leapt on to George's back, gripped the rim of the overflow and disappeared into it. Elsie followed, again using George's back as a stepping stone. Once in the hole, she wriggled round to hold a paw out to George, who jumped up and missed.

Uncle Vince's heavy footsteps came down the stairs.

'Quick, George, quick!' Elsie squeaked.

Taking a deep breath, George stepped back and ran towards Elsie's extended paw. As he jumped up, Uncle Vince caught sight of him, gave a howl of rage and lunged at the sink. Elsie grasped George's paw and hauled him through the hole. Together they slipped down the greasy overflow pipe.

They weren't safe yet. Uncle Vince was determined to get his own back. If he couldn't have the hamsters, he was determined that they shouldn't get away.

'I'll stop your little game,' he snarled.

Before they had slid round the 'p' bend, the hamsters heard a gurgling sound and smelled a terrible, choking smell.

Uncle Vince was pouring caustic soda crystals down the sink. He had filled the watering can with the long spout and was pouring water down the plug hole to dissolve the crystals into a burning fluid that followed the hamsters round the bend. Next, he blocked the opening to the overflow. First he stuffed in an oily, evil-smelling rag, then, for good measure, he drove in a wedge of wood.

'That'll stop you,' he snarled, dropping the plug into its hole and listening with satisfaction to the groaning and gurgling in the pipes. He began to search the cellar for any other exits until he was satisfied that there was no way that a hamster could escape.

'Get out of there – if you can!' he said.

8 Flood

Frank had no time to think before he was swept off his feet. He struggled to keep his nose in the air, but time after time the water sucked him under. Twice he struggled to the surface again, but the water was like some live thing, tugging him down and pulling him along.

'The others!' he thought. But that was all he had time to think as the water swirled and boiled around his head, filling his nose, mouth and ears.

Worse still, it was disgusting, greasy water with bits of food floating in it which got into Frank's mouth and up his nose. He was drowning and being disgusted at the same time.

As suddenly as it had started, the rush of water stopped. Frank hit something hard. It was the side of another pipe which opened out into a wider space, and the water retreated to a shallow level.

Frank lay on his back for a moment, winded, in a pool of watery filth. He coughed, and an old bean flew out of his mouth. Then something hit him with a soft thud, something lumpy and very wet that turned out to be Chestnut.

'Gor blimey,' he wheezed, when he could speak. 'What – *oomph!*'

Chestnut too had been hit by Maurice. Maurice was in a sad state, covered in bits of egg and quite unable to talk. When Felicity and Drew landed on him, they did manage to pump out most of the water he'd swallowed. Drew clung to Felicity's shoulders.

'That was fun!' he squeaked. 'Do it again, Mum!'

But poor Felicity was in no fit state to reply.

Frank struggled to his feet. The walls of the tunnel whirled briefly around him, then came to a stop.

'Is everyone here?' he gasped. 'Is everyone all right?'

'*All right?*' said Maurice, spitting out more bits of egg. '*All right?* That – was – the – very – worst – experience – of – my – life!'

'It was *disgusting*!' Felicity agreed.

'Oh, I don't know,' said Chestnut, nibbling on a piece of carrot. 'Bits of it were quite tasty.'

Felicity and Maurice looked as though they might be sick.

'I mean, is anyone seriously hurt?' said Frank. 'Can we all get up and get moving before it happens again?'

'Again?' cried Felicity. 'Where does all this filthy water come from?'

Frank looked uncomfortable. 'Well, sinks mostly,' he said. 'And, er, well, *some* of it from toilets.'

All the hamsters wailed and Chestnut spat out his carrot. Echoes magnified their voices until they nearly deafened Frank.

'Well, look,' he said. 'At least you're out of the Room Beneath!'

No one was impressed.

'I think I speak for everyone,' Maurice said, 'when I say that at the moment this hardly seems like a better option.'

'You've taken us from one death-trap to another,' Felicity said tearfully, wringing her paws.

'Personally,' said Maurice, 'I think I'd rather be skinned than drowned in people-poop.'

Frank glared at him. He was about to tell him that he was welcome to go back, when Chestnut spoke.

'Now look,' he said kindly, 'we've all had a terrible fright and I for one need to get my breath back. If we just rest up here a little bit, we'll all feel that much stronger and ready to go on.' He held up a paw as Maurice tried to speak. 'It's easy to complain,' he continued severely, 'especially when we're all in the dark. But this young buck knows what he's doing, don't you, Frank?'

There was a pause. Frank, of course, didn't have a clue, but he thought that this might not be the right time to mention it. Fortunately, Chestnut didn't seem to require an answer.

'He's brought us this far at Great Personal Risk, and I for one am right behind him,' Chestnut went on. 'And I'm sure when you've had time to recover, you'll all feel the same. Three cheers for Frank, that's what I say. Hip hip –'

No one cheered.

Felicity carried on clearing out Drew's ears.

Maurice looked furtive.

Frank looked away.

'Yes – well,' Chestnut said to Frank. 'Like I said, you give us a break now and we'll be right with you. Better have a rest yourself.'

Frank felt that they were wasting time, but he didn't have much choice. He was beginning to feel that being a Leader of Hamsters was an overrated thing. He left them all huddled together and went a little way along the pipe.

The floor of the pipeline was wet all the way along and at intervals great splashes dripped from above. These echoed quite loudly. The walls were running and slippery with water and it was some time before Frank found an opening where a lesser pipeline ran into this one. It was a network of smaller pipes leading to bigger ones. The pipe they were in should lead to yet another, bigger pipe, and so on until they reached the main sewer, which should run beneath the road where Mr Wiggs' pet shop was.

Frank found that he was forming an image of the system of pipes in his mind. 'It is a bit like the tunnelling of hamsters in the Wild,' he thought. And as horrible and frightening as the rush of water had been, it seemed to have taken them in the right direction much faster than they could travel. Another rush would carry them along even further. If they were really lucky, they might be swept all the way to the pet shop. All they would have to do would be to stay afloat.

These thoughts should have made Frank feel much better than he actually felt. In fact, he felt cold, hungry, battered and bruised. He was beginning to understand that being the leader meant being the person to blame. A small part of him wondered why he was trying to help these hamsters at all. And at the back of his mind he was very worried about Daisy, and Elsie and George – and even Mabel. Once he had seen this lot of hamsters to safety, he would have to go back to check on the others. At that moment it all seemed too much for one small hamster to do. Discouraged, he turned stiffly and limped back towards the others. Then he saw that Chestnut had come to meet him. The older hamster looked at him searchingly.

'Don't you take it to heart,' he said. 'They don't mean it. They were just shocked, that's all. Not used to adventure. Not like me.'

Frank looked at him. 'I thought you'd lived in the pet shop all your life,' he said.

'There's more than one kind of adventure,' said Chestnut. 'When I was young I was considered something of a tearaway. There was a big group of us – all young bucks – and we all used to get out at night and run amok. We used to torment the gerbils something terrible and run off with their food. We used to have major wars with the rats.' Chestnut shook his head, chuckling. 'Of course, old Wiggsy just got bigger and better containers to put us in – great big fish tanks made of glass, well-nigh impossible to get out of, but we found a way, oh yes. You'd be surprised. But these others, well, they've been used to a caged life – never been out of their cages before – so they're bound to feel a bit down, not like me. All this adventure makes me feel bold and reckless again, just like a young buck.' He cut a little caper for Frank, beaming, and Frank couldn't help smiling back. 'I thank you for that, I really do. And if you give the others a chance, they'll come round. You'll see. Sit down here with me a minute.'

Frank sat. He noticed that the others were gradually getting to their feet and grooming themselves. 'Maybe Chestnut was right,' he thought, and he began to groom his own pelt.

'You know what I've been thinking?' Chestnut asked. 'I've been wondering how it was that we could live in that room and not smell what was going on right under our noses.'

'It was that other smell,' Frank said, remembering. 'That sweet, sickly kind of scent.'

'Yes, but it didn't put *you* off. *You* could smell the danger.'

Frank shook his head.

'I don't know,' he said slowly. 'I think if I'd been kept there long enough I might have – well – kind of lost touch with my own instincts in a way.'

Chestnut nodded eagerly.

'That's it,' he said. 'It didn't just disguise the other smell, it *interfered* somehow, like some kind of drug.'

Frank nodded. That would explain the hamsters' peculiar behaviour.

'Well, I don't know,' Chestnut continued. 'All I know is, I've been remembering ever such a lot since I got out of that room with the funny smell. I can remember you, for instance, in the pet shop. I can remember you being born. I even remember your dam.'

All the fur on Frank's pelt lifted.

'My dam?' he said in a hushed voice.

'Leila,' Chestnut said, and there was a touch of reverence in his tone. 'She was a real beauty. Not golden brown like you, more grey. A lovely grey pelt like satin. She was in litter when she arrived. Old Wiggsy had no sooner got her in a tank when she had you – you and about seven others. Don't you remember?'

Frank shook his head. All he recalled about that faraway time was being bought by Guy.

'She hadn't long had you when someone bought her. I knew she'd be quick to go, she was such a beauty. It was sad for you cubs, though. You really don't remember her at all?'

Frank shook his head again, looking sad. 'Leila,' he thought. It was a musical sound.

'You were always such a bright, sparky little thing,' Chestnut went on. 'Always trying to get out when the others were fast asleep. I remember that young man that bought you – what's his name?'

'Guy,' said Frank.

'He kept coming and going, but he always came back for another look. And I said to myself, "He seems a decent sort of chap."'

'He is,' replied Frank, a little grudgingly.

' "That young cub'll be all right with the likes of him," I thought. But you really don't remember anything about when you were young?'

Once again Frank shook his head. 'It's too long ago,' he said gruffly. 'My memory doesn't go that far back.'

'But that's what I'm trying to tell you,' Chestnut said, his whiskers waggling in excitement. 'That's one thing I can do for you, now my memory's come back.'

Frank looked at him, uncomprehending.

'You can share mine with me,' he said. 'Haven't you ever done that before?'

Frank never had. Now that Chestnut had mentioned it, he knew that it was possible. He stared at the older hamster open-mouthed.

'Well, if you'd like to, that is,' Chestnut said. 'It's quite easy. You just sit with me, here, and sort of let your mind go blank . . .'

Hamster memory is not like ours. It is more of the body than the mind. If two or more hamsters get together they will begin to remember shared history or kinship patterns and even, if left long enough, the collective history of their tribe. Some people say that this is why they prefer to live alone, getting on with their own thoughts and memories without interference. It is even more remarkable, therefore, that when Uncle Vince kept Chestnut and the others together all that time, none of them experienced anything other than a deep forgetting.

Now Frank and Chestnut experienced a Shared Memory, of the pet shop with all its different animal smells and noises, and the scent of food. Frank had the impression of blurred light, and many cages. Briefly, he felt the sensation of being very small and weak, and being licked all over.

Then, in the centre of his mind, in the same place as he had perceived the silvery light, he saw her, very close, the softness of her fur, her dark eyes closed and opened, the whiskers quivered. He sat back, astonished.

It was as though he had always known her. 'Leila,' he whispered, and she seemed to smile, and once again Frank felt the intolerable coldness of her leaving . . .

. . . And he was back in the pipe with Chestnut. The others were watching them curiously now.

'Did you see her?' Chestnut asked. Frank could only nod, speechless. Chestnut squeezed his paw.

'Good for you,' he said. 'I'm glad I was able to help. It's sad when us hamsters get bought and sold and lose all contact with who we are.'

Frank found his voice. 'But that's exactly what I mean!' he said, quivering excitedly. 'While we're not free it'll always be the same. Bought and sold, kept in cages. *Skinned*. How can we know who we are? That's why I want us to start again, in the Wild! We could do it, Chestnut. We could start a tribe!'

For a moment there was a spark in Chestnut's eyes, then it died away and he shook his head.

'Maybe you could,' he said. 'But not me. I'm too old. Do you know how old I am?'

Frank didn't.

'I'm nearly three years old,' he said, and Frank was impressed. 'In the Wild I wouldn't have lasted this long. I've only got to this great age because of old Wiggsy looking after me. He didn't have to. He could have got rid of me when I didn't sell, but no, he kept me on. He calls me his old Chestnut,' the elderly hamster grinned, a gap-toothed grin. 'I miss old Wiggsy. And as for the others, well . . . The thing is, us hamsters are creatures of habit. We get fond of our Owners if they treat us right, and we like our creature comforts, so to speak. We're not really cut out for adventure.'

Frank wanted to contradict him, yet in his bones he could feel that Chestnut was right.

'Now and again a young buck like you, or me when I was younger,' Chestnut said, 'gets sparky and feels a stirring of the blood, and the call of the Wild. But that's not true of most hamsters, is it? I mean,' he said, nudging Frank as Maurice approached them, 'I can't really see Maurice taking to life in the Wild, can you?'

Maurice looked at them beadily.

'Are you two going to sit around talking all day?' he queried. 'Or are we going to get out of this awful place?'

Frank could see what Chestnut meant. He got up.

'We're ready if you are,' he said. He waited for Felicity and Drew to join them before explaining what he had worked out about the network of pipes.

As he did this, there was another gushing sound behind him as water streamed in from another tunnel. Both Maurice and Felicity moaned aloud. Frank spoke above the noise.

'Don't worry about the water,' he assured them. 'It's going our way. All we have to do is stay afloat and it'll take us where we want to go.'

'Or drown us,' Maurice said. 'It's all right for you, but I'm exhausted and my paws hurt. How do we know there won't be an even bigger flood next time?'

Frank didn't, but he wasn't going to waste time pointing out that there wasn't an alternative.

'I think we should just go,' he said firmly.

Chestnut said, 'Come on, Maurice. If an old codger like me can manage, a young buck like you shouldn't have any trouble at all.'

Maurice didn't look convinced.

Then Felicity spoke. 'Frank's right. We can't stay here forever.'

'That's a girl!' said Chestnut.

Drew jumped up and down and squeaked, 'More swimming, Mummy!'

So Maurice was outnumbered and fell in, somewhat sulkily, as Frank turned to lead the way.

They hadn't gone very far when once again the dirty water swept them up and flushed them along. The hamsters were less terrified this time. They understood that it only happened in short bursts. Also, now that they were in a bigger pipe it felt less like they were drowning. Even so, it wasn't at all pleasant. The water was murkier than ever and it was difficult to breathe. Frank kicked furiously to keep his nose out of it. Then, as the water drained away again, he realized that they were probably heading towards the biggest tunnel of all.

Beside him Chestnut swirled by gracefully in a little eddy, all four paws in the air.

'Here we go again,' he called to Frank. 'Try treading water. It's quite relaxing really.'

Drew gushed past and Frank could just see the tips of Felicity's ears.

'Swim faster, Mummy!' he squeaked.

Last of all, Maurice bounced off the wall and thudded into Chestnut. 'Grrrgle,' he said.

The water retreated, leaving behind a clutter of small objects. 'It was astonishing the things that got flushed down pipes, Frank thought. Cigarette ends and coins, small toys, bits of jewellery, even a set of false teeth that Maurice claimed had bitten him as they floated past. As the hamsters lay in a dripping heap, they could see that they were in a big, gloomy, echoing tunnel, filled with hollow rumblings. Maurice groaned and the echoes magnified his voice and reverberated round the tunnel so that he quickly fell silent. Drew squeaked and was rapidly hushed by Felicity. Chestnut sneezed and the sound was like gunfire.

Frank was the first to pick himself up. The water had retreated to a manageable depth and he splashed through it, trying to ignore the echoes. Was this, could it be, the main sewer that ran underneath the road where Mr Wiggs' pet shop was? And if so, how would they know which of the many pipes running into it would take them to Mr Wiggs?

Just then there was a muffled roaring overhead. Nearer and nearer it came, reaching a crescendo just above Frank's head, rumbling around the walls of the tunnel. Frank crouched, almost flattened, in the dirty water, before he scampered back to the others, who had huddled together in a dripping heap.

'Wh-what was that?' Felicity gasped, and the echoes gasped back at her.

'Traffic,' Frank murmured briefly. He did not want to set off too many echoes, or he could have explained to them all that he thought this was a good sign, a sign that they were approaching their destination. They all looked as though they needed a good sign, even Chestnut – exhausted, disheartened and petrified in varying measures. None of them liked the fact that they couldn't move quietly – the echoes would announce they were coming to any enemy a mile away. Being able to travel quickly and silently is one of a hamster's greatest assets, and without it even Chestnut looked lost and unsure of himself. Frank knew that if he didn't get them all moving they would enter that state that every rodent knows about and dreads – a state in which everything seems so alien and frightening that you forget, not only how to act, but who you are. Frank had been close to this state once before, in the Wild, so he knew how dangerous it was. He had to keep them moving, or they would just give up.

'Come on,' he whispered, with a confidence he didn't feel. 'It's only echoes.' His own voice whispered back at him eerily, but he set off anyway, with a firm step, looking back at the others. The first time he looked back no one had moved, but he kept going anyway, hoping to reassure them by appearing to know exactly what he was doing. After a moment Chestnut began to help Drew back on to Felicity's shoulders.

'Come on now, there's a brave lad,' he said.

Drew sniffed back his tears and the little group took the first few faltering steps along the tunnel, following Frank. Before long, water came again, carrying them along, but this time there didn't seem so much of it, or perhaps it was because the tunnel was so big. At any rate, it wasn't too hard to stay afloat and let it carry them along.

Once the water ebbed, Maurice began to recover sufficiently from his fear of the echoes to start complaining again.

'I shouldn't be surprised if I caught my death. I'm dripping wet and my paws hurt. I'm worn out. And where are we *now*, for heaven's sake?'

The other hamsters ignored him, splashing grimly on through the vast, dripping gloom. Maurice's voice rose and became even more querulous.

'I shouldn't be surprised if none of us ever sees the light of day again. Dragging us off to who knows where through some murky maze – full of germs and disease, I shouldn't wonder . . .'

Frank, plodding through the evil-smelling wet and cold, with the terrible rumbling noises from above, considered briefly whether he should go back and nip Maurice hard, but he was distracted by a new smell in the vast array of strange and unpleasant scents that assailed him. It was something he should know, he felt sure, something familiar. And whatever it was, it was getting stronger. He didn't like it.

Behind him Maurice's shrill tones ran on.

'. . . If we don't catch our deaths from all this freezing water, or drown, we'll end up riddled with diseases, you'll see. Don't say I didn't warn you. I – EEEK!'

Frank twisted round at the note of terror in Maurice's voice, just in time to see a black shape drop in front of him from the ceiling. Felicity squeaked in alarm as another dropped by her side. Then there were more and more of them, dropping suddenly and quite silently in spite of the echoes. The black shapes crouched then reared above the hamsters, monstrous and eerie, more than twice their size. Frank turned this way and that, but he was surrounded. He couldn't get to the others because two of the huge shapes blocked his way. Their stench filled his nostrils. At last he knew what they were: sewer rats.

The biggest of them leered down at Frank with a yellow grin.

'Well, lookee here, lads,' he said. 'Supper's arrived.'

9 George's Choice

The water churned and foamed in the pipe as it dissolved the caustic soda crystals, releasing a smell that burned the hamsters' nostrils and throats. It would burn the hides off them, too, they could tell, if it touched them. Faster and faster they slid along the slippery pipe, and plunged one by one into the water trap in the U-bend. The pipe gurgled and shook as the powerful liquid foamed behind them. Daisy plunged, unprepared, into the water of the U-bend with a little squeak of terror. She had no time to hesitate since Elsie was pushing her from behind. Once in the water, she struggled blindly, with no idea of how to swim round the bend. Elsie kept pushing, and behind Elsie, George dropped in. The combined weight of the two hamsters forced Daisy along, but ever so slowly. And the water continued to froth as the burning liquid dissolved in it.

Elsie pushed and kicked as Daisy broke the surface of the water then slid back in. Behind her, George could feel all the air being squeezed out of his lungs. Something terrible was happening in the water, he could tell. Already he felt weak and overcome. He could feel the stump of his tail burning. In front of him

Elsie gave an almighty thrust that propelled both herself and Daisy out of the U-bend and along the pipe. Then George surfaced, struggling and gasping, only to slide back in. Elsie paused.

'Go on,' George wheezed, surfacing again. 'Don't stop.'

He disappeared once more. Elsie backed up along the bend of the pipe.

'Grab my legs!' she called. 'George! George!'

There was no answer. Then she heard a choking gasp and felt George's paw clasp her hind leg. She pulled with all her might, hauling him over the bend. Then down, down they slithered, bumping into Daisy and round a final bend until the pipe levelled out and they were able to scramble along it to the little chamber they had reached before, with all the entrances to the different pipes. Here at last the air was clearer, though some of the choking fumes had followed them. Daisy wriggled round at once.

'George! Georgie!' she cried. 'Is George all right?'

Elsie collapsed, exhausted.

Daisy pulled George to the middle of the chamber and nuzzled him. 'George!' she kept saying. 'Oh, Georgie, Georgie!'

Elsie watched, askance. Daisy was all over George. 'Just as if *she* had saved him,' she thought.

'Oh, he's hurt,' Daisy sobbed. 'Oh, Georgie!'

'I'm all right,' George gasped. 'Just give me a minute.'

Daisy checked him all over, chafing his paws and licking his wounds.

'Oh, your poor tail,' she cried. 'Oh, does it hurt?'

There was a bald patch reaching from George's tail to right over his hindquarters where his pelt had been burned clean off.

'It'll be all right,' George said.

Slowly Elsie picked herself up. She felt a chill of loneliness as she watched Daisy fussing over George. They hardly seemed aware of her.

'Oh, Georgie, I was so scared. I thought I'd lost you!'

'Me too!'

The air was getting clearer all the time. Most of the burning liquid seemed to have been trapped by the water in the U-bend. Elsie looked round the little chamber, trying to concentrate. For the first time she thought of Mabel and wondered where she'd got to. Then she looked back at Daisy and George.

George was sitting up now, propped against Daisy, who was stroking him tenderly. He looked at Elsie and managed a tremulous smile.

'We made it,' he said huskily.

Elsie managed to smile back.

'Yes, George,' she said softly. 'We made it.' She cleared her throat. 'Now we have to think how to get back home.'

'I don't think Georgie is up to going anywhere right now,' Daisy said. 'He needs to rest.'

Elsie stared at Daisy. 'His name's *George*,' she said. She stopped herself from saying more harsh things. It was as though Daisy wanted to take over caring for George, which was Elsie's job. Long ago it had been

Elsie who had hidden him in her own cage, and groomed and trained him. She was his twin. It was on the tip of her tongue to say all of this, but George was looking at her pleadingly.

'I think I could do with a bit of a break,' he said.

Elsie sat down again.

'All right,' she said. 'But I shan't feel safe until I'm back in my own territory.'

She looked the other way as Daisy went on grooming George, and murmuring to him, and tickling him with her whiskers to make him laugh.

'Can you stand up yet?' she said. 'Come on, Georgie. Up on your feet. Like this.'

She did a limping little dance which made George laugh again and cough at the same time. Elsie looked at her coldly.

'What did happen to your leg?' she asked.

Daisy stopped dancing and her whiskers twitched.

'Why?' she said defensively. 'What's it to you?'

'No, go on, Daisy,' George said, propping himself up a little more. 'Tell us.'

'Well . . .' Daisy said reluctantly, then seeing that he really wanted to know, she began to tell them the story.

Unlike Chestnut, Felicity or Maurice, Daisy had once had an Owner. He had not been a very nice man. Not as bad as Uncle Vince, she added hastily, but still a nasty character. He had bought her because he wanted to train her for a hamster circus.

In no time at all he had Daisy strapped to a little trolley on wheels that he drove round the circus ring. He made her walk a tightrope by poking her along with a pin, and he had her clinging for all she was worth to a trapeze as he swung it back and forth. But it was when he attempted to fire her from a home-made cannon that the real damage had been done. Some mechanism inside the cannon had failed. When he lit the fuse there had been an explosion, but Daisy hadn't left the cannon. Instead both her back legs had been badly burned. The left one had recovered, but she had lost her right hind paw.

'Poor Daisy!' George said, trembling with indignation.

Elsie said, 'What happened?'

'Well, he took me back to the pet shop,' Daisy said. 'Back to old Wiggsy. Tried to tell him he'd been sold damaged goods, but Wiggsy wasn't having it. Then my Owner says, "You can have her anyway, she's no good to me." He pushed me across the counter and scarpered.'

There were tears of sympathy in George's eyes.

'It's all right!' Daisy said. 'Could have been a lot worse. Old Wiggsy took me back, though no one'd buy me from then on. He didn't have to do that so I'm grateful to him. I liked being in the pet shop better than being in a circus!'

Both Elsie and George were horrified at Daisy's story. Elsie felt a little ashamed of all the mean thoughts she'd had. She could see that Daisy was a very brave hamster who had learned to move nimbly and act as though being one paw short made no difference to her. But it still hurt that George was looking at her with so much love and sympathy, as if she was the only thing in the world that mattered.

'And really,' she thought, 'she's nothing but a performing beast.'

She cleared her throat again.

'Yes, well,' Elsie said, 'much as I'd like to stay here and listen to your life story, I really think we'd better be going.'

She felt as she said this that it wasn't a very nice thing to say, but then she realized that the other two weren't even listening. They were gazing at one another and clasping paws, and this made her cross all over again.

'I'm going to investigate these tunnels,' she said, when neither of them responded.

Elsie set off. She went a little way along the pipe immediately to her right, sniffing cautiously. She hadn't gone too far before she was shivering because of her fear of unknown territory. 'I wish Frank was here,' she thought. Frank liked exploring unknown places and she didn't at all. But she didn't want to give up too easily and return without having found out anything. The pipe was musty, but at least it was dry. Elsie couldn't detect anything that gave her the least clue where she was going. Discouraged, she was about to give up, when she was paralysed by a terrible noise – a high keening wail.

'*Eeeeeawwooo!*'

Elsie bolted backwards in terror. Daisy and George had heard it too and had leapt to their feet.

'What – was – that?' Elsie gasped, then it started again.

'*Eeeeawoooo*,' came the shrill wail.

Daisy and George clung to one another.

'What it is?' Daisy asked, trembling.

'It is I,' droned a spectral voice, 'the Black Hamster, calling you.'

Elsie, George and Daisy looked at each other in horror.

'The B-black Hamster,' Elsie stuttered. 'Wh-what shall we do?'

'Come to me now,' moaned the voice.

The hamsters looked desperately at the other pipes. They would have to run away down one of them, but which one?

The voice came again, louder now, as if approaching.

'Come to me,' it howled. 'Come to me or I – *oww!* Help!'

There was a rumbling, tumbling, crashing sound and a series of squeaks.

'Oww! Help?' said George. 'That doesn't sound like the Black Hamster.'

'Help! Quick!' squeaked the voice. 'The pipe's falling in!'

Elsie and George looked at one another.

'Mabel!' they said.

It was indeed Mabel. She had waited for a long time for Elsie and George to return, becoming first bored then cross.

'What *are* they doing?' she thought, and 'Typical, they don't think of anyone but themselves!'

Mabel wasn't an adventurous hamster and she didn't really want to explore. After waiting for what seemed like a long time, she eventually turned and stomped along one to see if she could find her way back.

'I bet they've gone home without me,' she thought. 'Just typical!'

One by one she tried all the pipes, not daring to venture too far. She wasn't good at trusting her instincts, like Frank, and at any rate hadn't had much practice. After getting wet once or twice, she decided she didn't like exploring at all. She returned to the little chamber. Finding herself safe and dry for the time being, she had curled up and had a little nap. She awoke to the sound of the other hamsters scurrying frantically along the pipe in her direction.

'They've been gone ages,' she thought. 'I'll teach them a lesson.' She disappeared quickly into one of the tunnels on the right. She had expected them to start searching the tunnels straight away and waited, hatching her wicked plan to frighten them all by pretending to be the Black Hamster. Mabel didn't really believe in the Black Hamster, but she knew that the others did. She had almost tired of waiting when Elsie entered the tunnel. This was her cue and she projected her loudest, spookiest voice.

Unfortunately she had made the pipes vibrate, and dislodged some of the surrounding earth and mortar, which fell through the cracks in the pipe. She had picked one of the older pipes and it had suddenly collapsed.

'Help me!' she squeaked, but this only made matters worse. There was another fall of mortar, and Mabel was trapped beneath the landslide.

'Help,' she moaned. 'George, Elsie, please!'

George hurried to the entrance of the pipe.

'I'm stuck in the pipe,' Mabel called.

Elsie bristled.

'Leave her there,' she said, feeling snappier than ever after her fright.

But George was already making his way into the pipe, towards the sound of Mabel's voice.

'Hang on,' he called.

'Hang on?' said Mabel peevishly. 'I'm *stuck*!'

'Do be careful, George,' said Elsie anxiously.

Daisy cried, 'Georgie, don't!'

But George was already tugging at the lumps of

mortar and clay. A little shower of shale shot out of the entrance as he kicked it backwards.

'Give us a hand, you two,' he grunted.

'As if,' said Elsie and Daisy together.

'Oh, come on,' said George. He reappeared at the entrance, covered in grey dust, and sneezed. 'I'm nearly through.'

'I don't even know why you're helping her,' said Daisy, and for once Elsie was in complete agreement.

'I heard that,' Mabel called. Elsie pushed past George into the pipe. There was Mabel, trapped beneath a heap of crumbled pipe. She didn't look hurt, so much as wedged. And sorry for herself.

'Oh, my poor legs,' she moaned.

'Serves you right,' said Elsie.

'Oh, that's right,' whimpered Mabel. 'Turn your back on me now, why don't you. Just abandon me here.'

'Good idea,' said Elsie and she turned and went back. 'I don't know why you're wasting your time,' she said, crawling out of the pipe into the chamber. 'You'll never get her out from under that lot.'

'We can't just leave her there,' said George.

'I don't see why not,' said Elsie. 'After all she's done. She's –'

But George was already climbing back into the pipe, followed by Daisy.

'What are you doing?' Elsie demanded. 'Why are you helping *her*?'

'I'm helping *him*,' Daisy said.

Elsie stuttered in fury, but it was no use. There was

a series of scraping noises and thumps, then another shower of mortar.

'*There*,' said George as he dislodged a big piece.

'Oooh, that's better,' said Mabel.

Then Daisy and George both began tugging her free. Elsie walked away from the entrance to the pipe and waited.

'Calm down,' she told herself. There was really no point getting this upset. Mabel would always be Mabel. She would always make trouble, and then when she got into trouble herself she would always expect someone to get her out of it. And someone like George always would because, well, because he was George.

Finally, a very dusty, crumpled Mabel was helped out of the pipe by Daisy and George. She limped ostentatiously to the centre of the chamber's floor and sank down.

'Oh, my paws,' she complained. 'I'm all dusty and wet.'

'Are we ready?' Elsie said. 'Can we get on now?'

'Oh, not just yet,' Mabel said. 'I have to recover.'

'You've held us up long enough,' Elsie said. 'Aren't you going to thank George.'

'I knew *he* wouldn't desert me,' Mabel said.

Elsie ignored this.

'Are we going to discuss what happens next?' she said.

'Not until I've had a rest,' said Mabel.

Elsie turned on her.

'You keep out of this,' she said, and there was something in her tone that made George and Daisy jump. 'You've been nothing but a nuisance from the start. If you hadn't held us all up when we were trying to get away from Uncle Vince, Daisy wouldn't have been caught in the first place. And you wouldn't go and rescue her, would you? No, that was up to George and me. But instead of finding your own way back, you lurk around in the pipes playing silly games and trying to frighten us all. Then when you get yourself stuck, *we* have to rescue *you*. You're nothing but a wicked, selfish beast!'

Mabel looked very angry at this. She started to rear up but staggered backwards instead, and had to content herself with saying, 'That's a fine way to talk to your own mother!'

Elsie nearly exploded.

'How dare you!' she said when she could finally speak. 'How dare *you* call yourself a mother! When have you *ever* acted like one? Have you told Daisy what you tried to do to your own cub – the same cub that you now expect to rescue you? Has she told you she tried to *eat* him?' she said to Daisy, who looked appalled. Elsie turned back to Mabel. It seemed as though all the anger she felt, about Uncle Vince, about George and Daisy, and about being trapped in the drains, was turning itself on Mabel. 'Didn't mention that, did you? And now, *now*, you expect us to wait for you. Well, I hope you've got some good reasons why we should.'

'Oh, go eat a worm!' said Mabel rudely, turning her back.

'Ladies, please,' said George. 'This isn't getting us

anywhere. Elsie's right, we have to discuss what happens next – and – and – I have something to say.'

Mabel and Elsie both looked at George. Daisy stood very close to him, horrified by what Elsie had told her. George waited a moment, as if he couldn't quite think how to tell them what he had to say, then he took a breath.

'The thing is,' he began, 'you're both anxious to get home. And I think I've got a plan. Mabel isn't in a fit state to go all the way to the other end of Bright Street on her own. So I've been thinking . . .'

He paused.

'Elsie and Mabel should go back together. Elsie –' he raised a paw as Elsie started to protest – 'You only live next door. When Lucy sees Mabel she'll recognize her and take her back to Tania's.'

Mabel smiled unpleasantly.

'Isn't that nice,' she said. 'We'll be just like dam and cub.'

Elsie ignored her.

'And you?' she said in a strange voice. 'Won't you be coming with us?'

George found it hard to look at Elsie. Instinctively his paw reached for Daisy.

'Well – we want – that is – I . . .' He stopped hopelessly, then began again.

'I mean we – well . . .'

By now Elsie knew exactly what he was going to say. As his twin she'd had close mental bonds with him since birth. They had shared memories and even dreams. Now it seemed to her that she'd known all along what he was going to say, and she felt a dreadful, hollow, sinking feeling. However, she was going to make him say it.

But George couldn't. He stuttered and rambled, until finally Daisy did it for him.

'Me and Georgie,' she said, lifting her chin defiantly, 'we're going to live together. In the Wild.'

A short silence was broken by a peal of contemptuous laughter from Mabel.

'In the Wild?' she said. 'Have you both gone mad?'

Elsie couldn't take her eyes away from George. He looked both guilty and relieved.

'It's for the best, Els,' he said. 'Daisy and me, we've not been happy with our Owners. I could take her back with me, but who knows what would happen? We'd probably end up being separated. And we, well, we want to stay together.'

And he exchanged such a look of love and pride with Daisy that Elsie could hardly bear it. She turned away.

'So that's it, then,' she said in a peculiar, strained voice. 'You've both decided.'

'Both gone squeaking mad, you mean,' said Mabel. 'They've been listening to that Frank. And he was *born* mad.'

George went up to Elsie and touched her shoulder, but she didn't turn round.

'It's for the best,' he said gently.

'For the best?' Elsie said, and now she couldn't keep the bitterness out of her voice. 'I'll never see you again. And that's for the best?'

'You could – come with us,' George said hesitantly, because he knew it would never work. Behind him Daisy was furiously shaking her head.

For an instant another kind of life flickered in Elsie's mind. A life in the Great Wild, where she and George and Daisy would live courageous and free. Together they would burrow and hunt. She would be aunty to lots of little cubs.

But Elsie had never felt a serious urge to go into the Wild. She was treated very well by an Owner who loved her and whom she loved in return. She missed Lucy and wanted nothing more than to return to Lucy's bedroom, and her old routine. Except that now there would be no George.

'I'll miss you,' she thought.

Just as if she had spoken the thought aloud, George stroked the back of her head. 'I'll miss you too,' he said.

Elsie wanted to burst into stormy tears and beg him not to go, but he had already turned sadly to Daisy, and they were holding hands once more.

Mabel said, 'Well, this is all very touching. But if you've quite finished, I want to get going. The Wild!' she snorted, shaking her head. 'You've been listening to a mad hamster, and where will that get you? Where is he now, eh? Probably already met his Doom. Still, each to his own. Let's go.'

Elsie's throat ached and she couldn't trust herself to speak. She started to follow Mabel.

'Elsie, wait,' George said. 'How will you know which pipe to follow?'

Elsie wouldn't look at him. She kept herself stiffly turned away from him. 'As if you cared,' she thought bitterly.

'Oh, didn't I tell you?' Mabel said. 'I've found that out.'

'You have?' asked George.

'Yes. Well, you left me here long enough,' Mabel said. 'I had to do something to pass the time. Look, it's easy. Elsie lives next door and her pipe's the next one along. Your pipe'd be the next one to that, if you were interested, which you're obviously not. My pipe's that one over there, but I think I'll stick with your plan. I don't fancy following a filthy drain for miles. I'll go back with Elsie. So, there you are. Simple really.' She beamed round, expecting praise.

'Well, you seem to have it all worked out,' George said, and paused. He was speaking to Mabel, but he was looking at Elsie. 'So that's it, then. Me and Daisy'll follow the main drain out beyond the houses, and try to find our way from there into the Wild.'

He pointed towards the direction they planned to take, but Elsie still wouldn't look.

'Wish us luck, Els,' he said quietly, but in a tone that tore at Elsie's heart. She felt as though the pipes were collapsing around her. She almost hoped they would, to ease the pain she was feeling. She hated Daisy and she could not, *would not*, give one word or look that would make it any easier for them to leave.

'You won't need luck where you're going,' Mabel said airily. 'At least, not for long. Owls'll soon get you. Or the foxes.'

Elsie pushed past her a little roughly. 'Let's go,' she said.

George's eyes misted over.

Daisy stroked his shoulder. 'We'd better get going too,' she said. 'Are you ready?'

George watched as Elsie entered the pipe, stiffly erect, still not turning round. Daisy took his paw. He cleared his throat.

'She was good to me,' he said. 'She was the first person who was ever really kind. She helped me when I needed it. She saved my life.'

Daisy nuzzled him.

'We'll be good to each other, Georgie,' she said. 'We'll help each other. You'll see.'

George smiled at her through his tears. Quickly, he dashed them away, and washed his face briskly, which is a hamster's equivalent to blowing his nose. Then he managed a real smile.

'I'm ready,' he said, and paw in paw they entered the biggest pipe, which would take them to their new life in an unknown world.

10 Battle

'Well I never,' said the biggest rat, who stood closest to Frank. 'If it ain't a little pack of pouch-stuffers.'

'Can we eat 'em?' said another.

'We can try,' said a third

'We can eat *anything*,' said a fourth, and all the rats agreed.

'We *can* eat them, of course,' said the biggest rat. 'But what I want to know is: what's a little pack of pouch-stuffers doing down here. On our territory. Offering themselves up like bait?'

Frank said nothing. He could think of nothing to say that might improve the situation, so he kept quiet. The biggest rat had a long lean face and long yellow teeth. He looked mean and hungry in equal measure, and he smelled bad. Of course, the fact that they were all in a sewer meant that none of them smelled good, exactly, but what Frank meant was that they didn't smell friendly.

'Courage!' he thought, but it only helped a bit.

'Lost your voice?' asked the biggest rat in mock concern. 'Did it get washed away?'

'Can you squeak?' asked another, and he gave

Maurice a little push. Maurice squeaked loudly, which amused the rats no end. They pushed him again and he squeaked some more. The rats copied him and the tunnel echoed with their eerie laughter.

'Right, that's it,' said Chestnut, incensed. 'You've gone too far now. Tell them, Frank.' He took up a fighting stance. 'You take that one and I'll take on these two.'

The rats shrieked with mirth. It was a chilling sound.

'Leave it out, Grandad,' one spluttered. 'You're killing me. And it's our job to kill you.'

Frank had had enough. He drew himself up to his full height, which meant, depressingly, that he was about half as tall as the biggest rat.

'Fellow rodents,' he said clearly, 'I'm asking you to grant us way-leave.' (This is the way that one animal may ask another for permission to pass through its territory.)

There was a further gust of laughter from the rats. 'Fellow rodents!' they echoed, nudging one another.

Frank ignored them and went on, his heart hammering. If he said just one thing wrong he knew they would pounce.

'We don't want trouble,' he said, groping for the right words, not too grovelling, not too bold. 'We have a cub with us. We are taking him to a place of safety. We ask your permission to carry on.'

Silence. But it was the silence of the hunting animal watching prey.

Frank licked his lips. 'So, if you don't mind,' he said, 'we'll be going.'

'Not so fast,' said the biggest rat. 'Nobody passes this way without tribute. What do we get out of it if we let you go?'

Frank looked him in the eye. 'Our gratitude,' he said firmly.

The rats fell about.

'That's a good one!'

'Never heard that one before!'

'What do you think, Tyler,' one said to the biggest rat. 'Shall we let them go? Or shall we eat them?'

Tyler grinned and all the rats started squeaking at the hamsters, a chilling sound that echoed through the tunnel like demented laughter – or a war-cry. Felicity clutched Drew and huddled closer to Maurice and Chestnut.

Frank wasn't going to cower. He went on staring at Tyler until gradually the squeaking stopped. Then he said, 'Well, much as we'd like to stay around and amuse you some more, we have to be going.'

'Not so fast,' said Tyler. 'You don't know these tunnels like we do. You can't go wandering around them without an escort. They're dangerous, aren't they, lads?'

The rats agreed.

'Full of nasty characters,' said one.

'You meet some very funny types,' said another, and all the time they were forming a circle round the hamsters. Frank could hear the others whispering behind him.

'We're trapped.'

'Oh, whatever will we do?'

'This is the worst mess yet.'

Suddenly he felt really cross.

'Right,' he said to Tyler, and the rat's eyes glowed. 'If you want a fight, you've got one.'

'*Ooooh!*' said all the rats.

'But let the others go!' said Frank.

'Aaah, in'e sweet!'

'Good speech, good speech.'

'What do you think? Should we let 'em go?'

'Nah.'

Behind Frank one of the rats grabbed Drew. Felicity emitted the loudest war-cry Frank had ever heard and launched herself at the rat. Frank glanced round, taking his eyes off Tyler for the first time, and Tyler stepped forward and cuffed Frank smartly to the ground.

Frank heard a roaring rush in his ears. He leapt up, incensed, only to be cuffed to the ground again. Tyler was playing with him, he knew – he hadn't even started to bite yet.

The next few moments were rather blurred. Frank bounced up again and sprang at Tyler, sinking his teeth into the rat's soft underbelly. The rat howled in pain, which gave Frank some satisfaction. Then two other rats pulled him off and held him while Tyler sank his teeth into the back of Frank's neck. To his left, Chestnut was grappling gamely with a smaller rat and shouting 'Oi! Leave him alone!' while another rat had Maurice backed up against the wall.

Yet more were passing Drew around above Felicity's head.

Summoning his best Lightning Twist Propulsion Manoeuvre, Frank tore himself out of the rats' grasp and launched himself again at Tyler, hitting him full on the belly. Tyler rolled over with a sound like you would get if you punched an airbag. Frank landed on top of him, biting and clawing for all he was worth. If he had to die, he thought, he would die fighting.

Tyler released another agonized yowl, and immediately another rat was on Frank, biting and tearing. Chestnut launched himself at that rat and another rat threw himself on Chestnut. The rest was a blur of teeth and fur.

Things were not looking good for Frank. He was being bitten and mauled from all sides and the combined weight of rats was crushing him. Even so, he managed another good bite (hoping it wasn't Chestnut) and several kicks. All hamsters can fight if they have to, and Frank's blood was up, so he hardly cared that they were losing, borne down by unbearable odds . . .

'Well, well, well,' said a voice, clear above the chaos. 'What've we got here?'

From his position underneath three rats and a hamster, Frank couldn't see a thing. Slowly he felt the pressure release as the rats got up, and the chaos around him subsided. A squeaking whisper ran through the group.

'Rolf!'

'It's Rolf!'

'Rolf!'

Chestnut still lay across Frank, panting. He seemed to be trying to say something, but he was winded. Slowly Frank heaved him off. And there, behind all the other rats, and rearing above even Tyler, was the biggest rat Frank had ever seen. He was the size of a guinea-pig (Frank could just remember guinea-pigs from his time with Mr Wiggs) and his effect on Tyler's gang was impressive. Some of them had already run away, and Tyler was cowering.

'I asked a question,' the enormous rat said in his enormous voice.

'Leave it out, Rolf,' Tyler said, but not as if his heart was in it.

Rolf stepped towards him and Tyler visibly shrank.

'We found 'em first,' Tyler said petulantly. 'It's not fair! They're ours.'

Rolf's voice was dangerously low.

'*Yours?*' he said. 'Have you forgotten our little agreement?'

Tyler shuffled from one paw to another.

'*All* the booty in this part of the tunnel,' Rolf kicked at a fallen rat, 'is mine.'

'Oh, great,' Frank thought. 'He just wants to kill us himself.'

'Now, I told you what would happen,' Rolf went on, 'if our little agreement was broken.' He stepped over the fallen rat and with one swift movement had the struggling Tyler pinned to the floor. Then he looked up and, if a rat could be said to bark, he barked at the remaining members of Tyler's gang. 'Get out of my sight!' he said. 'NOW!'

The rats fled. Frank saw Rolf take hold of Tyler's jaw and twist his head round, further, further, until Frank thought his neck must surely break.

'And as for you,' Rolf said, his voice low and even again, 'I don't want to see you, hear you, or smell you, in this part of the tunnel, ever again. Is – that – clear?' With each word he gave Tyler's neck a further twist, then suddenly released him. With a strangled gasp, Tyler hobbled away as fast as he could.

Rolf turned to the hamsters. Just as Frank was trying to work out whether, if they all took Rolf at once, they could possibly get past him, the most surprising thing that had happened yet on this very surprising and eventful day happened then.

Felicity ran towards the enormous rat. He leapt towards her and they nuzzled.

'Felicity!' he said.

'Oh, Rolf!' said Felicity. 'I thought I'd never see you again!'

Frank thought he must have taken a blow to the head. Nothing was making sense. He clambered slowly to his feet, astonished. Beside him Chestnut struggled to his feet as well, and Chestnut was beaming.

'I've been so worried about you!' Rolf was saying.

Felicity said, 'I'm so glad to see you, so glad!'

Frank stared at them as they clasped each other in the dank and dripping tunnel. 'What –?' he began, bewildered. Then, 'Who –?'

'That's what I've been trying to tell you,' Chestnut wheezed. 'That's Rolf.'

'Who's Rolf?' Frank whispered back, but Chestnut was hobbling over to the big Rat and shaking his paw. Then he hugged him, and Rolf patted his shoulder.

'Who's Rolf?' Frank demanded again, looking at Maurice.

All Maurice would say was, 'That great brute *sat* on me. I think I've broken my ribs. Are you sure they've all gone?'

Then Chestnut detached himself from the little huddle and came back to Frank, still smiling mysteriously as though something really special had taken place.

'Who is he?' Frank said yet again. 'What's going on?'

Poor Chestnut looked very bruised and battered. His whiskers were matted with blood and one ear was hanging off. Still he was grinning broadly.

'What a fight!' he said to Frank. 'Just like the old days. Did you see me take that great brute on?' He did a little dance with his fists up. 'First, a hook to the jaw, then in with a right –'

'Will someone tell me what's going on?' Frank almost shouted.

'Shhh!' Chestnut said, glancing over his shoulder to where Felicity and Rolf were still nuzzling each other. He drew Frank and the whimpering Maurice aside conspiratorially. 'Rolf's an old friend,' he said in low tones. 'He's a –'

'Troublemaker,' Maurice put in waspishly. 'Wherever he is, trouble follows.'

Chestnut looked reprovingly at Maurice.

'Are you going to let me tell Frank or not?' he said with dignity.

'Yes, let him,' Frank said impatiently, and Chestnut began.

It seemed that Rolf was not a wild rat at all. He had been born in Mr Wiggs' pet shop – the biggest and noisiest of a litter who fought and squabbled and generally made trouble. No one bought them. They just got bigger and more troublesome. They got out of their cages at night and set all the little gerbils free and chased them away. They stole the hamsters' food or bullied them into giving it to them. They let the water out of the fish tank. And they fought each other and Rolf always won. He even fought the cat. He caused so much damage that eventually Mr Wiggs had to keep him on his own in a sealed container.

'No one'll buy my rats if they look like they've been fighting,' he said. And so Rolf was kept on his own, peace was restored and everyone was happy.

Except for Rolf, that is, who began to look wild and strange. He stopped eating and grooming himself. Sometimes he would butt his head against the glass container, then roll over, biting himself when he failed to get out. None of the other rodents knew what to do. They thought he might be going mad, but they worried that if he was set free he would start causing trouble again. So weeks passed. Other rodents came and went, but Rolf stayed, looking wilder and more unkempt until no one would have anything to do with him.

Then one day Felicity was brought in. Because she wasn't part of a group of hamsters, and she was expecting babies, Mr Wiggs gave her a cage of her own, next to Rolf.

'How do you do,' she said to Rolf. Felicity was a very polite hamster. But Rolf just snarled. 'Oh dear,' Felicity said. 'Whatever's the matter?'

'What's the matter with this poor rat?' she asked the other hamsters. In hushed tones so that Rolf wouldn't hear, they told her the tale.

'But that's terrible,' Felicity said. 'He'll make himself ill.'

And so she began to talk to Rolf in gentle, soothing tones, ignoring when he snarled or spat. She told him stories and even sang songs. Gradually, as the days passed, Rolf began to listen. She sang him to sleep every morning. When he woke in the night, if she wasn't awake, he would tap on the wall of his container until she woke up and told him a story. He began to eat, and to keep himself clean.

The other hamsters didn't approve. Relationships between different kinds of rodent were strictly forbidden in their code of conduct. Hamsters kept to themselves, mice and gerbils looked after their own, and everyone knew rats were a law unto themselves. Most of the hamsters, apart from Chestnut, began to shun Felicity, but she didn't mind. It seemed as though she and Rolf only cared for each other.

One weekend, Mr Wiggs and his wife went away, leaving the shop in the hands of their nephew, Gordon.

'Check all the cages last thing,' Mr Wiggs told him. 'And keep the cat out.'

But Gordon was more interested in playing cards with a group of friends he'd invited over. He forgot entirely about replacing the special seal round Rolf's container, and he left the cat in the shop. Around midnight the cat had the kind of mad fit that cats sometimes have. She ran around the shop as though pursued by wolves, knocking over containers of food and dog biscuits and toppling Rolf's container to the floor. In a second Rolf was free, facing the cat, who crouched low, staring at him, her tail twitching from side to side.

'Rolf!' squeaked Felicity, rattling the bars of her cage. All the hamsters watched in terror.

Rolf did the only thing he could. Instead of waiting to be pounced on and eaten, he leapt at the cat, landing full on her face, and sank his teeth into an ear.

The cat yowled and ran around the room in a frenzy, all her fur standing on end so that she looked like an enormous striped brush. Felicity clutched the bars of her cage, hardly able to breathe.

Rolf dropped off, but the cat kept running, leaping

up to the small open window at the back of the shop, through it and along the street, still yowling.

Then Rolf climbed up to Felicity's cage.

'Felicity, I'm free!' he said.

'Oh, Rolf,' she panted. 'You were so brave!'

'I can't stay here,' he said. 'Come with me, Fliss.'

'Don't do it, Felicity!' the other hamsters chorused.

'I'll take care of you,' Rolf said. 'We have to find somewhere we can be together.'

Felicity's eyes filled as she looked at him. 'I can't,' she said.

'Why not?' said Rolf. 'Don't listen to them. I thought you loved me.'

'I do,' Felicity said. 'But I can't just think about myself.' She changed position slightly, exposing her underside, so that Rolf could see that, any moment now, she would have her litter.

Rolf stared at her in silence. This was his only chance to escape. He could see that Felicity was in no condition to follow him. He clutched the bars of her cage.

'Felicity, I *have* to go,' he said.

Felicity nodded, tears dripping from the end of her nose and running along her whiskers.

'You must go,' she said. 'Oh Rolf, I'll think about you every day.'

Rolf clasped her paws through the bars and they nuzzled briefly.

'I'll never forget you,' he whispered.

Then he was off, scrambling over the counter and

jumping from it to a ledge which led to a pipe running the length of the wall to a small grille. There he turned and craned his neck to see Felicity one more time. Felicity too tried to stand and stretch upwards so she could see him, but the counter blocked her view.

'Goodbye, my Fliss,' he called, and he squeezed through the bars of the grille and hadn't been seen again. Until now.

'We all thought he was dead,' Chestnut said. 'Felicity was terribly upset. But she had her litter. Even when most of them were sold, there was still baby Drew to keep her going. And, well, we all thought that it was probably for the best and that she'd get over him.'

Frank looked again at Felicity and Rolf, who were still clasped together.

'It doesn't look like it,' he said.

Maurice said, 'Absolutely disgusting, if you ask me. It's not natural.'

'No one's asking you,' said Chestnut.

Frank went over to the happy couple.

'Er, hello,' he said.

Felicity turned. 'Oh Frank,' she said. 'Rolf, this is Frank. He saved all our lives. Frank, this is my dear, dear Rolf.'

Rolf extended a paw to Frank.

'Felicity was just telling me about you,' he said. 'You're a hero, mate.'

Frank took the huge paw a little awkwardly. He had never shaken paws with a rat before.

'You're the hero,' he said. 'Thank you for saving our lives.'

Rolf put his paw back on Felicity's shoulder.

'Isn't she beautiful?' he said.

Felicity blushed.

'Oh Rolf, I look terrible,' she said, fishing some sewage out of her pelt.

'Not to me,' said Rolf. 'You'll always be beautiful to me. I thought I'd lost her,' he said to Frank. 'Now I've found her again, I'm telling you. I'll never let her go.'

'He's my new dad!' squeaked Drew, bouncing up and down.

Frank blinked at them. 'What do you mean?' he said.

'She's coming with me,' said Rolf. 'I've got my own place now, and I'm taking her there. And little Drew, of course.'

By this time Chestnut and Maurice had joined them.

'You can't do that,' Maurice said, scandalized, though he kept well behind Chestnut and Frank. 'Hamsters don't live with rats!'

Felicity looked at him and there was a gleam in her eye.

'Well, I'm going to live with Rolf,' she said firmly.

'But how will you live, down the sewers?' asked Chestnut.

'Don't worry about that,' said Rolf, 'I know my way around. And I'll take good care of them, never fear. No harm'll come to them while I'm around.' He squeezed Felicity quite fiercely.

Maurice started to say, 'Your place is with your own kind . . .' but he tailed off, muttering, when he caught the expression in Rolf's eyes.

'My place is with Rolf,' Felicity said. 'We belong together. I'd rather live in a sewer with him than in a comfortable cage without him.'

Frank could see that they meant it. He looked at them wistfully. They were going to live for themselves, without cages or Owners. It was what he had always wanted. Chestnut stepped forward and clasped Felicity's paw.

'Well, I think it's marvellous,' he said, sounding quite choked up. 'Good luck to you both.'

Felicity and Rolf shook paws with Chestnut and Frank. Chestnut picked baby Drew up and petted him. Maurice stood aloof, muttering darkly.

'Well,' said Chestnut, putting Drew down and wiping a tear from his eye, 'that's you sorted, then. All we've got to do now is to find our way back to the pet shop.'

'Oh, that's easy,' said Rolf. 'You're nearly there. I'll take you, if you like. We'll be going that way.'

'Really?' said Chestnut and Frank together.

'I go past the pet shop's pipe all the time,' Rolf said. 'Because some of the food gets flushed down. It's not far.'

Chestnut looked at Frank. 'Well, if we can go with Rolf,' he said, 'there's no need for you to take us. Unless you want to see the old shop again.'

Frank thought about the pet shop where all the animals lived in cages and shuddered slightly. 'Not particularly,' he said.

'Don't blame you, mate,' said Rolf. 'There's no need. You can set off back home if you like.'

Frank didn't especially want to go home either. But he did want to find out what had happened to Elsie, Daisy and George.

'If you're sure,' he said doubtfully.

'Sure I'm sure,' said Rolf. 'I'll make sure Chestnut and old prune-face there get back safe and sound. You leave it to me.'

'I beg your pardon,' said Maurice.

'Granted,' said Rolf.

'But what about the other rats?' Felicity said. 'Frank can't fight them on his own.'

'Don't worry about them,' said Rolf. 'The word's out now. No rat'll come near.'

So it was settled. The hamsters shook paws with Frank, Felicity kissed him, Drew clung to his neck and Chestnut hugged him and said he must be sure to visit them some time, and they all thanked him again and again. Even Maurice said, somewhat sourly, that he was thankful Frank had managed not to kill them all on the way. Then they all set off, following Rolf. Frank watched them until they had almost disappeared into the gloom, with a queer feeling of loneliness.

At the last moment, Chestnut turned and waved.

'Take care of yourself, old son,' he called. 'Keep your paws up and your whiskers clean. Fight the good fight.' Whatever else he said disappeared into the echoes.

Frank was alone. He had to find his own way back. He had set out with eight hamsters and now here he was, alone again in the enormous tunnel. 'So much for leading a tribe,' he thought. But he knew there wasn't time to reflect. There was still work to do, and he had to set off while he had some strength left. 'Courage!' he told himself, and the faint spark that was in him glowed once more.

It was hard to remember how far they'd come, but Frank trotted on, following the scent they'd left. A hamster's nose is a very useful instrument, as are the hip glands they use to release a scent that marks out territory. Frank could have followed the trail for miles, so he didn't feel lost. But he had forgotten one vital thing.

As the trail approached the next sewer he heard the sound of water gurgling in the pipes. 'Bother,' he thought. He prepared to tread water once more. It seemed like a large torrent this time and Frank wasn't sure how far it would take him. Then he stopped, struck by a terrible thought.

The water would carry him away from where he was going! However hard he tried to get back along the narrower pipes, it would sweep him back into the main sewer. He couldn't swim against it. It would gush over him and sweep him further and further away, until he was lost, or drowned.

The pipes thundered as the churning torrent approached. Remembering the rats, Frank made a desperate attempt to climb the walls of the sewer, but they were slippery with water and slime. He watched in horror as the biggest flood yet foamed out of the other sewer and swept towards him with terrifying speed.

'So this is it,' the calm part of his brain thought. 'This is how it all ends.'

11 Help!

The roaring of the water filled Frank's head as he stood directly in its flow. Deafened, he could hardly think. He closed his eyes.

'Help,' he thought. It was the only thought that came clearly into his mind. He tried again, without even knowing who he was asking or what he was asking for.

'Help,' he thought again.

Then the water was all around him.

'So much for help,' he thought, and prepared to drown.

Slowly he realized he was perfectly dry.

Very cautiously, Frank opened one eye.

What he saw astonished him so much that he opened both eyes and stared.

The water was all around him. Or, to be more exact, there was a wall of water far taller than Frank himself on either side of him. In the middle, ahead of Frank, was a long clear, dry path.

It wasn't possible.

Frank blinked.

The path was still there.

Frank didn't understand. He could hardly make sense of what he was seeing. His heart beat fast. Nervously he licked his lips. On both sides of him the waters surged, but in front of him there was a dry path.

There was only one thing to do. He put out one trembling paw, then another, and stepped forward. The waters might close over his head at any instant, but there was no point thinking that. Tentatively, as if in a dream, he walked between the walls of water, slowly at first, then gathering speed.

On Frank trotted, round the bend and into the next sewer. Still the path was clear and the waters did not close over his head. Frank didn't like it but there wasn't a choice. Someone, or something, was keeping him safe. He could only hope that it kept on keeping him safe until he got home.

Gradually the sound of the water changed. There was a wave-like gushing on either side of Frank which continued for several moments while Frank trotted furiously on. As he entered the next, narrower tunnel, it seemed to him that the waters were less high. A wave of water poured forward then retreated, again and again. He could see over the water now and this spurred him on. He entered the next pipe and the water spurted along at his side, finally dwindling to a trickle. Soon, with a final spurt, it disappeared, as though draining down a sink.

Panting for breath, Frank paused and looked behind him, watching the water disappear. It was incredible – the strangest thing he'd ever seen. But he couldn't think about that now. He had to think about where he was going.

And then he realized that the path through the water had brought him all the way back to the small chamber where all the pipes began. Ahead of him was the pipe that would take Frank back into the Room Beneath. Frank trotted forward, then paused. There was something funny in the air. A peculiar choking smell that he hadn't noticed before was coming from the pipe. Frank went up to the entrance and sniffed it cautiously. It didn't smell good. It smelled like danger. As he sniffed the inside of his nostrils began to burn and he retreated quickly.

Frank didn't know what to think. As far as he knew, his friends might still be in the Room Beneath. Uncle Vince might have caught them and they might be in terrible danger. Or – but Frank didn't allow himself to think the word 'dead'. He had to get to them. As he approached the pipe again, the smell wafted towards him and he reeled back, choking. Something bad was in the pipe and he didn't know what it was. It smelled like poison.

Taking a deep breath, Frank tried again. This time he got part way into the pipe, but he was soon forced to retreat, coughing. His whiskers felt singed. What was he going to do? He glanced round at the other pipes. If he followed one of them, perhaps he would still be able to get into the Room Beneath. He sniffed the other exits. There was no burning smell in them as far as he could tell. But which one should he try?

Something had got him this far, so perhaps it

would help him again now. 'All right,' he thought. 'Which way?'

Nothing.

Then, as Frank peered into each of the pipes in turn, he felt a small blast of air from an exit he hadn't noticed before, near to the pipe with the burning smell, but set higher in the wall. He stretched up to peer inside it, and he thought he saw a faint glow a little way along it. He poked his nose in and stared and sniffed.

There it was again, a faint glimmer, like the tiny column of flame he'd seen before, only this time the glow was softer, like a luminous dust. It gave off no smell, and it didn't seem connected to the burning in the other pipe. It hovered ahead of him, almost as if beckoning him in. He had to follow it.

Frank set off, pursuing the tiny glow. He scrambled over the rough wet surface of the pipe. The pipe climbed steeply and Frank could tell that he wouldn't emerge into a Room Beneath. As he travelled steadily on it occurred to him that this pipe might take him to the sink in the kitchen of Uncle Vince's house.

Up and up Frank climbed. When he came to a U-bend full of water he realized he was probably correct. Without hesitating, he plunged into the water. By now he was quite practised at kicking his way through water. Here there was more of it than in the U-bend from the Room Beneath. His lungs were bursting as he wriggled round the bend. Thrusting upwards, he broke the surface of the water. Here, as before, the pipe branched. Frank turned into the pipe that curved round and led him to the overflow of the kitchen sink.

The tiny glow seemed to have disappeared, now that he knew where he was. The pipe was narrow, but hamsters are good at pushing themselves through narrow places – which was fortunate, because the overflow hole itself was much smaller.

Frank didn't stop to think. He had to keep up the momentum of his pushing. He kicked and squeezed and struggled, grasping the rim of the overflow to pull himself through. It felt rather like pushing himself through a mangle, as though the whole shape of his body was changing as he squeezed it through the small opening.

Finally he emerged, squashed, breathless and bedraggled, into a blinding light. He slid unceremoniously into the sink with his eyes tightly shut, aware only of the need to find shelter . . .

. . . And the next moment something large and heavy descended around him. It was a glass jar and the insides were sticky with jam.

'Well, well, well,' breathed Uncle Vince. 'What have we got here?'

Frank tumbled backwards into a pool of jam as Uncle Vince scooped up the jar. Before he could struggle to his feet, the lid was screwed on. Uncle Vince's voice sounded strange through the glass.

'Have you come to visit your Uncle Vincey, then?' he said. 'Well, he's very glad to see you! Oh yes.'

Uncle Vince's voice was not only strange because of the glass. It sounded as though he'd been drinking, or as though, brooding on the failure of his plans for the other hamsters, he'd gone a little mad.

'We'll just have to take you into our special room then, won't we?' Uncle Vince continued, in the same unnatural voice.

Frank clawed frantically at the sides of the jar. It was an extra-large jar of Supa-Cheap jam from the shop where Jackie worked. Frank recognized it because Guy bought it as well. It was big enough to stand up in and it still contained substantial amounts of jam that dripped on him now as Uncle Vince held the jar upside-down. Jam trickled down Frank's ears and along his back. The smell was overpowering. Uncle Vince unlocked the door to the cellar.

'Come and see what I've got for you,' he said in a peculiar sing-song voice as he went down the stairs.

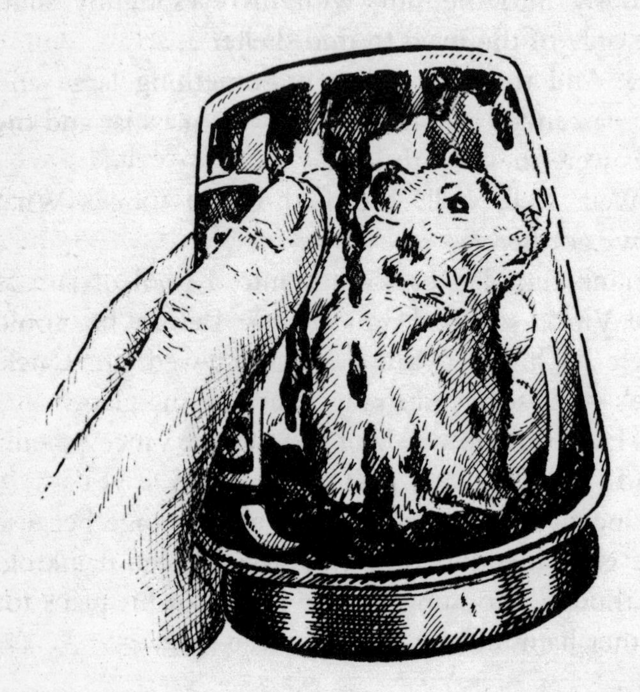

Frank pressed his paws against the sticky glass, trying in vain to see out. The next moment the pouchy, stubbly face that was by now horribly familiar was peering back at him.

'Ex-cel-lent,' Uncle Vince murmured. 'A fine specimen for your Uncle Vincey. Strong and meaty, yes. A little bit messy, though. Hamster jam!' He tittered. 'Best clean you up first. Must have you looking your best for Uncle Vincey.'

He placed the glass jar on the table. Frank heard a snapping, popping sound as Uncle Vince blew out the fingers of a pair of rubber gloves and drew them on. Frank pushed against the glass, trying to topple the jar, but it was too big and heavy. And though he strained to see, there was too much jam on the sides. The smell, mingled with the terrible smells of the Room Beneath, made him feel quite sick.

'Now for the tweezers,' Uncle Vince said, holding them up reverently. 'And some intzy-wintzy swabs. There we go! And – where did I put the chloroform?'

Frank could just about make Vince out as he held up different bottles to the light so that he could read the labels. He could see that there were a lot of objects on the table apart from him, including the large, covered thing he had seen before, mysterious and lumpy. Further than that he couldn't see, and he couldn't think of a single thing to do. He had run out of ideas, and he had run out of time.

Then, as he pressed his nose to the sticky glass, he saw Uncle Vince draw the cover off the huge object that occupied most of the table. He gasped as the gleaming machinery was revealed – the pulleys and wheels, the blades. Vince switched it on and it swung smoothly into motion. The conveyor belt moved and the blades sliced down. The true horror of Frank's situation came home to him. This was the machine Uncle Vince would use to skin him! Soon he would be pegged on the line with all the other skins.

'Mustn't forget the pegs,' Uncle Vince said.

He picked up the jar, turned it over again so that Frank slithered down the sides, and unscrewed the lid. He tipped Frank out on to the bench and immediately caught him, holding him a little too tightly in his fist. Frank struggled and bit, but his teeth closed on rubber, not flesh. Uncle Vince smiled, revealing broken yellow teeth.

'Oooh, bit of a fighter, are we?' he murmured. 'Perhaps we'd better have a little sniff of this.'

Using the tweezers he held in his other hand, Uncle Vince picked up a swab of cotton wool and dunked it into some powerful-smelling liquid. Then he wafted the swab backwards and forwards over Frank's nose.

Frank felt the urge to fight draining away. He felt weak and ill. Uncle Vince's huge face swam before him and he closed his eyes.

Uncle Vince took the swab away and tied Frank loosely to the same board that Daisy had been secured to earlier. Frank became aware, through all the alien and revolting smells that swam in his senses, of a different presence in the room. A different scent, old and wild, yet strangely familiar, overwhelmed all the others. It was all-encompassing, vast. Frank struggled to open his eyes, then stared.

There, behind Uncle Vince, and towering above him, was an enormous black hamster. It was *the* Black Hamster, Frank would have known him anywhere, straight away. However, the last time he had seen him, he had been just a bit bigger than Frank, and now he was *immense.* He filled the room, vast and dark as night. His eyes glowed red and his teeth were huge.

And Uncle Vince hadn't realized yet.

'There you are, little hamster!' he said. 'We'll just get you tied down properly and then we'll start.' Stubby fingers pressed Frank into position. 'Now, where did Uncle Vincey put the cord? It's here somewhere. Is it under this pot? No. Well, it must be in this box. No. Then it can't be all the way upstairs, surely? It must be here somewhere . . .'

And muttering to himself, fingers groping among all the objects on the table, Uncle Vince finally turned round.

12 What Josh Saw

Meanwhile, another day had started on Bright Street. Jake, Josh and Thomas were sitting on Jackie's settee. They had been sitting there all week, she told them. It was the first week of the holidays and they had hardly moved.

'There's nothing to do,' Jake said.

'Of course there is,' said Jackie.

'I want to play with George,' said Josh.

Jackie sighed.

'We all miss George,' she said. 'But there's no point brooding about it. If you'd go out and play you might forget about him for a while.'

'Can we have a dog?' asked Jake.

'No,' said Jackie.

'Khalid's getting a dog,' said Jake.

'Well, go and sit on his settee, then.'

'But why can't we?'

'Look,' said Jackie, straightening (she had been trying to fix the vacuum-cleaner). 'I know you're upset about George. But you didn't really take that much notice of him when he was here. I was always the one who cleaned him out and looked after him. So don't tell me it'd be any different with a dog. Go on out and play.'

But Jake, Josh and Thomas just wanted to sit on the settee looking fed up. Jackie started to change the plug on the vacuum-cleaner.

'Just look at you lot. I don't know. Looks like we all need cheering up. What we need round here is a party,' she said.

'*Yeah!*' yelled Jake, Josh and Thomas, and they began jumping around.

'A fund-raising party,' Jackie mused. 'To raise funds for the school.'

'*Awww!*' said Jake, Josh and Thomas, but Jackie was thinking.

'We could have a street sale,' she said, 'with pop and balloons.'

'YEAH!!' yelled Jake, Josh and Thomas. 'Can we have a clown?'

'Get off the settee,' said Jackie. 'We could have a party *and* raise funds. You know there was all that vandalism at the school last month. And we could collect signatures for a lollipop lady at that crossing. And you can sell off some of your old toys.' She saw their faces. 'Oh, don't worry,' she continued, 'it'll be fun as well. We'll get the whole street involved. And I'll sort out the party food. But there's one condition – you have to go out and play!'

Jackie put the vacuum-cleaner away as Jake, Josh and Thomas finally left. The more she thought about it the more it seemed like a good idea. Everyone had been down since the break-ins. Jake and Josh had insisted on sleeping with Jackie every night, and even the neighbours who didn't have hamsters were nervous. 'It would be a good idea to brighten everyone up,' she thought, and she went out right away to knock on the neighbours' doors.

She didn't have much luck. The curtains were always closed at number 1, so she didn't bother knocking. Lucy's mum, Angie, was in the bath. When she knocked at number 7, Mrs Timms's house, no one answered, even though the curtains twitched and two of her many cats rubbed up against Jackie's legs.

At number 9 Arthur kept Jackie talking for quite a long time, about Jean's arthritis, his sciatica and the collection of war memorabilia he'd inherited from an uncle.

'Maybe you could bring it to the sale?' Jackie said.

Arthur looked alarmed.

'Oh, I don't mean to sell it,' she reassured him. 'You could just show it to the kiddies. They'd be fascinated.'

Arthur promised that he'd think about it, and Jackie went on to number 11. But Tania was out with Lucy and her mum and dad, so, feeling rather deflated by now, Jackie knocked at Guy's door.

Guy answered, looking pale and distracted. He was holding a bucket in one hand and the grill from a grill pan in the other, and he had one of those lamps that cyclists sometimes use at night strapped to his forehead.

'Frank's gone,' he said. 'He must have got out last night. I've been looking everywhere.'

'Oh no!' said Jackie, and she went in with him to

look. 'Oh my goodness,' she said when she saw the state of Guy's front room. 'They've really trashed it!'

Guy looked blank. 'Who?' he said.

'The burglars,' said Jackie. 'Haven't you called the police?'

'Oh no – that's me,' Guy said. 'I've been looking everywhere. I don't understand it,' he said, rubbing his nose with the grill. 'I was with him all the time. I even slept down here.'

Jackie was very sorry to hear that Frank had gone. She would have helped Guy to look, except that there was so much stuff overturned in his living-room that she couldn't think where to start. Instead, she told him that she had to get back. He looked so stricken that she stood on his doorstep for a while, telling him about the street sale, and he told her about his Infallible Plan for catching hamsters, which involved the grill and the bucket. The headlamp was so that he could see behind cupboards and under the floor.

Meanwhile, at the other end of Bright Street, Josh, Jake and Thomas had started to play football.

'But I don't want to be in goal,' said Josh.

'It's your turn,' said Thomas.

'It's always my turn,' said Josh.

'That's because you can't kick,' said Jake.

'It's not fair,' said Josh. 'I want a go.'

'No!' said Jake and Thomas.

'I'm not playing, then,' said Josh.

'Baby,' said Jake.

Josh was mad. Thomas and Jake were always ganging up on him and they always won because they were older. He went off by himself, kicking a stone along the pavement. Past Thomas's house he went, dribbling the stone just like the captain of the England team. Then, in front of number 1, it rolled into the gutter and fell with a plop down the grating.

'Goal!' said Josh, looking around, forlorn.

The curtains were pulled across the window of number 1. They were always like that, even in day-time. It was daft. 'Maybe the man who lived there was a vampire,' Josh thought.

If you stood to one side of the window you could just see through a chink where the curtain had been pulled too far over. Josh stood on tiptoe and peered in.

At first he could see nothing, it was too dark. But if he pressed his face right up against the glass and squinted sideways, he could see something. He could see ...

Hamster cages!

Josh stood back from the window. At the other end of the street he could see his mum, still talking to Guy. He squinted through the window again. 'Mum,' he said. Then, 'Mum! *Mum!*'

Jackie came running, thinking that Josh must have hurt himself. Behind her, Guy stepped on to the street, still carrying the grill and bucket and wearing the headlamp, and Jake and Thomas left off playing football.

'What is it?' Jackie said, breathlessly. 'What's wrong?'

'Look, Mum, look!' said Josh, so excited he could hardly speak.

'What? What are you looking at? Oh Josh, you know you shouldn't look in people's windows.'

Josh jumped up and down with excitement.

'Look, Mum – hamsters!'

'What? I can't see.' Jackie pushed Josh to one side and squinted along the length of the window.

Jake, Thomas and Guy ran up to join them.

'It's dark,' Jackie said. 'I can't see if –'

Then she straightened, her face pale.

'Call the police,' she said.

13 The Black Hamster Returns

Uncle Vince's face changed colour from a bruised purple to a grisly yellow. He opened his mouth to scream, but only a kind of rattle came out. He seemed paralysed, clutching the tweezers in one hand, the other flung up before him as if for protection.

Then, in a voice as deep as the bowels of the earth and as old as time, the Black Hamster spoke, and the language he used was human.

'Vincent,' he said, and a kind of shock like a thrill ran through Frank. 'Why do you persecute my people?'

He extended a gigantic paw and tweaked the tweezers from Uncle Vince's hand.

'You won't be needing these any more,' he said.

At last Uncle Vince found his voice.

'*AAAAAAAAAAAAAAAAAGGGGGGGGHHHHHHHH*,' he said.

He ran all the way round the table and fell up the stairs. (It is not easy to fall *up* rather than *down* stairs, but if you had seen him you would know exactly what I mean.)

Still tied loosely to the board, Frank wriggled and kicked.

'Get him!' he shouted. 'Don't let him go!'

The Black Hamster lowered his enormous nose towards Frank and he bit through the cords that tied Frank to the board.

'I don't think that will be necessary,' he said, in hamster this time.

And in fact it wasn't. For, just as Uncle Vince stumbled into the front room, there was a loud rap at the door. When Uncle Vince opened it there were two policemen, with Jackie, Guy and the boys jostling anxiously behind.

'Where's my hamster?' Guy shouted, very red in the face.

To everyone's surprise, Uncle Vince threw himself into the arms of the first policeman, babbling about a gigantic talking hamster, as tall as a tree.

'Of course he is,' said the policeman, patting Uncle Vince's shoulder. 'And my Uncle Bertram's a cockatoo. Now, perhaps you'd like to come with me to the station and have a nice cup of tea.'

Meanwhile, in the Room Beneath, the Black Hamster picked Frank up in his enormous paws.

'Hold on,' he said.

There was a sudden, dramatic plunge, the dimensions of the room seemed to change. Frank felt himself turning over, the wind whistling through his ears . . . and he was at floor level, or not quite. He was clutching at something soft but strong . . . He was standing on the back of the Black Hamster!

The Black Hamster had reduced himself to roughly twice the size of Frank, and Frank was clutching his shoulders! He could feel the thick, velvety pelt in his paws, the thrum of blood.

'How – how did you –?' he started to say.

But the Black Hamster said, 'Hold on,' again. And they were off, running directly towards the back wall, gaining speed ... and just as collision seemed imminent, the wall before them gave way and they were running, not through the wall cavity of a small terraced row called Bright Street, but through the vast plains and windy deserts of Syria. Frank could see the same strange, exciting rock formations he had seen the last time he had travelled through the Spaces Between – tall pillars of rock, colonnades, and carved statues.

Still clinging to the shoulders of the Black Hamster, Frank had the impression of a vast network of passages, tunnels in the rock leading to an infinite labyrinth of burrows, and to great pillared halls – halls where the ancient lore of hamsters had been passed on for thousands of centuries since the world began. Frank felt the wonder and glory of this place, in the heart of the Desolate Wastes, a monument, it seemed to him, to hamster ingenuity and courage.

The Black Hamster slowed to a walking pace. Frank breathed it all in as though he couldn't get enough – the reddish sandstone, hewn and shaped by centuries of tunnelling, the mysterious carvings on the pillars. Here his ancestors had lived and thrived. He was descendant of the same race that had carved this stone. Red light glowed on the carved rock, and the whole of that immense city seemed suspended in silence. Frank couldn't help but register the eerie emptiness of the empty halls, the hollow burrows. The wind blew a flurry of dust from a half-finished statue, and Frank felt a powerful ache of belonging and loss.

'What happened here?' he said, his voice carried by a melancholy echo.

The Black Hamster paused and Frank got down.

'What is this place?' Frank asked, though he already knew the answer. This was Narkiz, the Ancient City, centre of the original territory of hamsters, also known as Narkiz, that stretched for miles beneath the Syrian sands.

'What happened?' he asked again.

The Black Hamster looked at him with eyes that contained an inexpressible sadness.

'Man,' he said.

The single syllable hung on the air, and in that moment Frank had a series of fleeting images – the appearance of human civilization, mud villages with disease and squalor, then the coming of great machines.

Frank turned to the Black Hamster, bemused.

'Is it gone?' he whispered.

The Black Hamster bowed his head until his nose nearly touched the desert floor. And indeed it was gone, for all Frank could see around him now was wall cavity, and he could smell, unmistakably through the plaster, the scent of Guy's front room.

Frank whirled round quickly to make sure that the Black Hamster was still there.

'No' he said. 'Not yet!' He had too many questions to ask, about Narkiz, and about things that had happened on the journey, the parting of the waters, the pillar of flame, and the Room Beneath, where the Black Hamster had appeared in gigantic form. And about where he went to when he left Frank, and what he wanted Frank to do. And what about Elsie, and George, Daisy and Mabel – what had happened to them?

The Black Hamster reached forward and touched his nose briefly to Frank's. The sense of electricity made all his fur stand on end.

'Your friends are safe,' he said. 'They don't need you any more.'

Frank moved fast. He clutched at the velvety pelt, but found that his paws were empty.

'Don't go,' he cried sharply.

The Black Hamster looked at Frank quizzically. Frank struggled to find what he wanted to say.

'You left me before – all that time – and I didn't know what to do – you never *told* me – you just went.'

There, he'd said it. He looked up defiantly, but the Black Hamster just stared back at him with the same half-quizzical, half-humorous expression. Into Frank's mind rose the memory of the gift he'd been given, of communication with Guy, and how he'd used it. Without wanting to, he had an image of the time he'd made Guy eat an entire bowl of hamster food.

'You seem to have been busy,' the Black Hamster's voice said in Frank's mind, and Frank understood that he'd been too busy playing foolish games to fully understand the nature of his power, or his quest. And he understood also that when he really needed the Black Hamster, rather than just wanting to see him, he would be there. But now he was fading.

'I won't do it again,' Frank called. 'Come back!'

But there was just an impression of the Black Hamster, like a shadow on the wall.

'Help my people,' the shadow said, and then it vanished.

Frank felt foolish, and cross, especially with himself. And he felt a desperate sense of longing for Narkiz. Yet he couldn't feel too heavy at heart, for the sense of the Black Hamster's presence was still with him, and the memory of the marvellous things he'd seen. He felt sure that he would see him again, even if for now he had to return to his old life with Guy. He glanced round and before him, in the crumbling plaster of the wall, there was a tiny crack. He nibbled and burrowed, following the unmistakable scent of a forlorn Guy, and finally he poked his nose out, just above the skirting-board. He climbed out in a little shower of plaster and dust, and sneezed.

'*Frank!*' squeaked Guy, sounding rather like a giant hamster himself. 'Franky, Franky, Franky!'

Frank allowed himself to be picked up.

'Oh Frank!' said Guy. 'Oh – *yuk*! Where *have* you been?'

14 Home Again

A big fuss was made over the return of the hamsters to Bright Street and to Mr Wiggs' pet shop. There were pictures in the local paper of Mr Wiggs beaming over a tank full of hamsters, and one of him shaking hands with Josh, with Jackie grinning in the background, as well as one of Uncle Vince looking mean in the dock. There was a photo of Mabel, as one of the hamsters who'd returned, stretched out luxuriously in her carriage with the little parasol, and one of the Room Beneath with the evil machine and the tragic little row of hamster skins still hanging over the table. 'Chamber of Horrors', the caption read. and Mr Wiggs had waxed eloquent over the hamsters who had never returned. There was even a quote from Mr Marusiak, saying that you never knew who you were renting to these days, and apologizing to everyone for the trouble he'd caused. There were no pictures of Frank, of course, since he hadn't been one of the hamsters taken and no one knew that he'd been involved at all.

Then, as suddenly as it had blown up, all the fuss was over. Things got back to normal. Frank was quite happy about this. He was exhausted after his big adventure and just wanted some peace and quiet. The main thing, as far as he was concerned, was that, because of public outcry, Uncle Vince was sent down for a long time. Jackie called round to tell Guy all about it.

Apparently Vince had been unemployed for ages, she said, and the strain had got to him. He'd had a number of jobs that had come to nothing. Then he had tried to set up businesses on his own, selling household items door to door, and mowing lawns. But he wasn't very popular, because, Jackie said, he looked too suspicious. Then he had turned to inventing things, but one way or another they weren't very practical. He'd invented a satellite dish for motor bikes so you could watch Sky TV as you cruised along. The traffic police weren't amused. And then he'd invented an automatic poop-scoop to use when dog-walking. This ran into problems when it was discovered that it was actually pushing the poop back into the dog.

So, eventually, he'd run out of both ideas and money. He had taken to sitting in all day, reading an assortment of odd magazines that he took from doctors' or dentists' waiting-rooms when no one was looking. In one of these, *Fur and Feathers Gazette*, he read an article that said that hamster was the new ermine. It was then that he'd conceived his evil plan. When he'd found that number 1 Bright Street was for rent, near a pet shop, he'd taken it right away. It was an added bonus to discover that so many hamsters lived on Bright Street itself. He bought a second-hand sewing-machine, installed it in the cellar, and set to work right away on developing his monstrous machine. He'd also read a lot about chemicals, especially anaesthetics, and had come up with the idea of mixing a little with scented oils to keep the hamsters drowsy and quiet, because if a hamster gets very stressed and anxious its pelt will deteriorate. It may even develop 'wet tail', a very messy condition. Uncle Vince wanted to make sure that all the pelts were tiptop, so he'd looked after all the hamsters – before skinning them, that is.

'Well, thank goodness he was caught before he did any more damage,' Guy said. 'And thank goodness he didn't get Frank. Though where Frank did get to I don't know. He was *filthy*. I had to shampoo him and dry him with a hair-dryer – he seemed to be covered in *jam*!'

'At least you got him back,' said Jackie, looking sad. 'I don't know what's happened to little George. The kids really miss him. You know Mr Wiggs gave Josh a year's supply of hamster food, because we all thought we'd get him back once Uncle Vince was caught. So, now we've got a huge sack of hamster food and no hamster. Jackie's eyes filled with tears. 'I just wish I knew he was all right,' she continued, blowing her nose.

Frank knew that George probably was all right. After he'd settled in a bit and had a good long sleep, he'd nipped next door to Mabel's house, partly to make sure she was safe, and she'd told him scornfully that George had gone off with Daisy.

Frank could hardly believe it. George? In the Wild?

'I don't know why you're so surprised,' Mabel said grumpily (she seemed grumpier than ever after her adventure). 'I thought that was all part of your Grand Plan. "Hello, I'm Frank and I want you all to come and live with me in the dirt and eat worms." '

Frank could see she was not in the mood for conversation, so after asking about Elsie ('Don't talk to me about that little minx – what a temper!') he'd gone back to his cage, puzzled and a little envious. George and Daisy in the Wild! Who knew where they were now? 'Probably dead,' Mabel had said, but Frank didn't think so. For one thing, the Black Hamster had told him that all his friends were safe, and he was sure he would know, somehow, if any of them needed help. No, George and Daisy would be busy making a new life for themselves, he felt sure, just like Felicity and Rolf.

In fact, almost everyone had a new life except for Frank. He had helped them, and now he was back in his cage in Guy's front room. But he tried not to feel too sad about this. He thought, when he got his strength back, that he might go and visit his friends in their new homes and that would be an adventure in itself. Meanwhile, he had a lot of working out to do, about his Quest, and what the Black Hamster had said about helping his people. Somehow, Frank knew he had to sort that one out for himself.

But here was Jackie, still very upset, on Guy's settee. And Guy had moved closer to her, and was patting her shoulder awkwardly.

Alarm bells went off in Frank's mind. He could see

now that Guy definitely liked Jackie, and the horrible prospect of Guy and Jackie getting together hovered before him. It might mean that he would have to live with Jake and Josh!

'No way,' he thought, and instantly took control of Guy's mind. Absent-mindedly Guy reached for a cheese and chutney sandwich. He rolled it up in his fingers and pushed it into his left nostril. Then he did the same thing with his right nostril. Jackie sat up very straight.

'What *are* you doing?' she said.

Guy leaned forward and dunked both the sandwiches into his cup of tea, then snorted them up his nose again noisily.

'It's really nice,' he spluttered, spraying Jackie with cheese and tea. 'You try it.'

Jackie was already half way to the front door.

'Oh Guy,' she said in alarm, 'do try to get out more or you – you'll end up just like Uncle Vince!'

And with that she was gone, leaving Guy to pull the sandwiches out of his nose dreamily and eat them.

'What does she mean, just like Uncle Vince?' he said slowly, remembering. 'That's not nice, is it? What does she *mean*?'

And he carried on like this for some time, quite upset. Frank did feel a little guilty. Worse, he felt that he had once again abused his power, and that he wouldn't get anywhere unless he learned to use it the right way. But he didn't want any possibility of being transferred to number 5. He didn't even want Jake and Josh coming round to number 13 to play with him now that George had gone. No, he had done the right thing, he told himself firmly as he curled up in his bed – or at least, the best he could. Guy would just have to get himself another girlfriend, and that was that.

It took Jackie some time to organize the street party. First, there was a week of relentless rain, then Tania and her mum and dad were away. When they came back, Arthur and Jean went to their caravan in Wales for the weekend. Jackie began to despair of finding a day when everyone would be there and the weather was fine. Eventually, some weeks after the hamsters returned, the right day dawned.

The sale was a great success. It was a cloudless day, and a lot of people came by to look at the different things set out on the tables – clothes and toys, bric-à-brac. Even Mrs Timms was persuaded to sit out in one of Arthur and Jean's folding chairs and look through Arthur's war memorabilia.

Jackie had made jellies for the children, and bought crisps and pop. Thomas and Lucy's dad, Des, brought some big shiny balloons from the factory where he worked, and Tania's mum made little fondant tarts. Tania and Lucy, who had fallen out, were on speaking terms again, both of them delighted to have their hamsters back. Jake and Josh looked rather glum, so to cheer them up, Des brought his Pride and Joy out of the backyard.

Des's Pride and Joy was a vintage motor bike, a Douglas Dragonfly called Duggie, with a Swallow sidecar. It had, as he explained to the baffled children, a high-compression engine, with competition gear ratios and a high-lift camshaft. He hadn't ridden it for years, his wife Angie said. He spent hours in the backyard cleaning and polishing it and fiddling with the gears. Today was a special day, Des said, and he entertained all the children by giving them rides around the waste ground in the sidecar.

Frank watched all this from a little table near Guy's window. He had instructed Guy to put his cage there so he could have a proper view. His view was a little obstructed by Guy, who leaned against the window chatting to Jackie. He was evidently attempting to make up for the last time they'd met.

'You know, about the last time,' Frank heard him say, 'when you came round –'

But Jackie wasn't listening. 'Who's *that*?' she said.

That turned out to be Des's friend Mick on his Matchless 500.

'Who is he?' Jackie said to Angie, and Angie said that Mick used to be Des's best mate, then Des had settled down but Mick was still on the road. He was known as Matchless Mick, or Matchless to his friends.

'He's *nice*,' Jackie said, and a dreamy look came over her face. Frank saw the look on Guy's face and felt sorry for him all over again.

Now all the children could ride round the waste ground at once, taking turns on the different bikes. Mick had brought beer for the adults, and after that the party was a great success. Arthur had a good time explaining his war memorabilia over and over again. Mrs Timms seemed happy to sit in the sun with Jean and a glass or two of beer, and Tania's mum sold a lot of her dried flowers. The children's toys, old videos and clothes went quickly enough and so did Guy's old guitar. He sold it to Matchless Mick and the two of them had quite a long conversation about being in a band. Mick made him play a few chords on the old guitar, and said he was excellent, and Guy decided that he wasn't a bad sort after all. In no time at all they were playing together and everyone sang, even Mrs Timms.

Then, most unexpectedly, Mr Wiggs turned up, carrying a mysterious-looking box. He had heard, he said to Jackie, that a certain young man's hamster had not returned, and he had come with a replacement.

And from the box he withdrew a clear container, and there inside it was a very worried-looking Maurice.

Frank grinned. 'Serve him right,' he thought.

Josh was speechless with delight.

'He was my hamster too,' Jake said jealously.

'Then he will belong to both of you,' Mr Wiggs said gravely, and there was much excitement.

'Yeah!'

'Wicked!'

'Cool!'

'Can we play with him now, Mum?'

'What do you say to Mr Wiggs?' Jackie said, and there was a chorus of thank yous. 'Go on,' she said to them, 'go and see if he likes George's cage. Look out for the cat,' she called after them. Frank's last glimpse was of a petrified Maurice with his paws pressed desperately against the walls of his container. Frank tried to feel sympathetic, but he couldn't help chuckling.

Mr Wiggs was persuaded to stay and have a beer, and Arthur showed him his war memorabilia. He even joined in the singing, which went on well into the evening, until it was quite dark. Everyone agreed it was the best street party ever, and they must do it again sometime. The adults cleared the tables and swept up the food, and the children lit sparklers. Everyone was tired, but happy.

Everyone apart from Elsie, that is. Elsie, though she tried to put on a brave face, was not very happy at all.

She was pleased to be back, of course, and Lucy had been thrilled to find her when she came back from her outing with Tania and her parents. Imagine their astonishment to find Elsie and Mabel together in the middle of the carpet, waiting for Lucy's return. They were beside themselves with delight. Lucy didn't want to put Elsie back in her cage. She played with her on her bed that night, and petted and fussed and groomed her. For the next few days, whenever she got in she ran upstairs to check on Elsie. She woke her by tapping on her bedroom with a cracker, then taking her out for exercise in her ball. And she always made sure there was something special in her bowl to tempt her. Because Elsie didn't seem to be recovering her appetite, and Lucy thought she was losing weight.

'What's wrong, Elsie?' she said. 'You don't seem really happy.'

Elsie tried. She capered dutifully on Lucy's palm to make Lucy feel better, but it was a rather half-hearted caper. She did feel a bit comforted when Lucy was there, but when she wasn't she just felt dreadfully sad. And most of the time she just wanted to go to sleep.

'She's probably still tired after being away all that time,' Lucy's mum said, comfortingly. 'Poor little thing. She'll perk up soon.'

But Elsie didn't perk up. As the days passed her whiskers drooped and her coat lost its sheen. She even forgot to keep her droppings separate from her food.

'It's not like her, Mum,' Lucy worried. 'What's the matter?'

The matter, of course, was George. Elsie missed him terribly. Even though she hadn't seen that much of him when he lived with Jake and Josh, she knew he was just next door, and there was always a chance he might pop in. She had thought, several times, of visiting him herself, but she was put off by the thought of the cat, and the Spaces Between. Now she felt more familiar with the Spaces Between, but George wasn't there to visit.

She had been so happy when she found him again. She had even adjusted to being in the strange house, without Lucy, because she was near George at last. Although she loved Lucy, the only time she ever felt that she really *belonged* was when she was with George. They had been cubs together, and that wasn't something you could forget.

But now George was gone.

He had gone into the Wild, where anything might have happened to him. He might be starving, or wounded, or lost.

He had chosen to go, and Elsie had chosen not to. She was quite sure that she didn't want to live in the Wild, or with Daisy, so she'd chosen to live with Lucy instead. And she didn't regret her decision, not exactly, but she did wish that she knew how George was – that he was safe, and looking after himself, and that, if he had to live with Daisy, she was being good to him.

Sometimes Elsie felt quite fierce when she thought what she would do if she found out that Daisy wasn't being good to George.

But the fact was, she had no way of knowing.

Sometimes Elsie thought that not knowing anything was worse than knowing that something bad had happened.

But what really made her feel bad was the way they had parted. She had let him go without saying a kind word, or wishing him well.

She hadn't even said goodbye.

This was the thought that came to her most frequently as she stared mournfully out of her cage at night, too dispirited to make her way out of the cage, as she used to, and forage. And this was the thought most likely to send a tear trickling all the way down her nose to the end of her whiskers, where it hung and quivered before dropping off. Days turned into weeks and nothing happened to alter the sadness that she felt.

Then, one night, more than a week after the party, something did happen.

Lucy had been unusually restless that night, but finally she had gone to sleep. Even the grown-ups had gone to sleep, and all the house was dark. So you would have had to have unusually good eyesight to see a small troop of hamsters heading across the living-room carpet in an orderly manner. If you had really good eyesight you would have noticed that it was George who was ushering some very tiny hamsters along, and keeping them all in line. If you had really good ears you would have heard him saying,

'Keep in line now,' and

'Watch where you're going,' and

'No pushing!'

When they got to the staircase he said, 'Now, all of you, pay attention. This bit's hard.' He helped them to climb on his shoulders one at a time, then balance on the wrought-iron railing and edge their way upwards, the way Elsie had shown him so long ago. On the top landing he led them past the bathroom, explaining what all the strange noises were, then past the main bedroom where Lucy's mum and dad snored together in a kind of harmony, then he made them all stop and look up at the ceiling and told them about the Boy in the Roof.

At last they came to Lucy's room, and the door, as usual, was open, just a fraction.

George squeezed his way in, followed by his tiny troop. All was quiet. There was only the sound of Lucy's regular, quiet breathing and the ticking of the clock. From time to time a beam of light from a passing car travelled across the wall and was gone, but nothing else disturbed them as George demonstrated how to climb the canvas curtain up to Lucy's desk. He had to give one tiny hamster a tug here, and another a push there, but he travelled up and down the curtain very confidently. Soon they were all on the desk top, squeaking a little in excitement at all the strange noises and smells, until George reminded them sternly to be quiet.

'Leave the toys alone,' he ordered two of the bigger cubs. 'We're not here to play, we're here to see your Aunty Elsie.' Then, 'I wonder if she's asleep,' he muttered to himself.

Elsie wasn't asleep, but she was in bed. She'd been having a bad night and couldn't get comfortable. Of course, usually night-time would be her active time, when she reorganized her cage and ran around her wheel, but these days she hadn't the heart. She had just decided to move her bed. As George approached she had her back to him, and she was so busy tugging at the strands of her bedding that she didn't even hear or smell anything unusual.

When George saw her his face lit up. He motioned quickly to all the little hamsters to be quiet, then crept right up to the cage. Elsie was so preoccupied she didn't even notice.

'Ahem,' George said, and Elsie jumped violently.

When she turned, her face went through an indescribable change. It was just as if an old sad tired face had been peeled off to reveal a different, younger face, filled with incredulous joy.

'*George!*' she breathed.

'Hello, Elsie,' said George.

Elsie took a faltering step forward and George pressed his paws up against her cage. She reached out as though to touch his face through the see-through panel.

'George,' she said again and her eyes filled with tears.

George looked quite emotional as well.

'I – ahem – brought you some visitors,' he said, and all the little hamsters crowded round.

Elsie was speechless.

'This is Dermot,' George said, patting a grubby, greyish one. 'And Danny.' He pushed one of the bigger ones forward. 'Donal, Declan and Dean. And this,' he said, picking up the littlest hamster of all, who had very pretty brown-grey fur, 'is little Elsie.'

'Oh George,' was all Elsie managed to say. Her

chin trembled. Then she remembered her manners. 'You must all be starving,' she said. 'Would you like something to eat?'

'Yes please, Aunty Elsie,' chorused all the little hamsters.

'I've got plenty of food in here,' Elsie said. 'Do you think you can help me get the lid off my cage?'

In no time at all the lid was off Elsie's cage and all the little hamsters swarmed inside, filling their pouches with the food Elsie had stored but not eaten. Then they ran around her wheel and played games in the sawdust chamber. Elsie and George watched them, laughing. Elsie shook her head.

'I must be dreaming,' she said. 'Oh George, I've been so worried. I didn't know where you were.' And she covered her face and wept while George patted her shoulder.

'Why is Aunty Elsie crying?' asked Dermot.

'I'm not crying really,' Elsie sobbed. 'I'm just so pleased to see you.'

'Run along and play,' George said to Dermot. 'Aunty and Daddy have a lot of catching up to do.'

Elsie wiped her eyes. 'Oh George,' she said, 'I missed you so much.'

'I missed you too, Elsie,' said George, and for a moment it looked as though they might both cry, but Elsie pulled herself together.

'All these cubs!' she said.

'Six,' said George proudly.

There was so much to say.

George told Elsie that he and Daisy had found

their way into the Wild with few problems, and they had dug a burrow for themselves right away. They were busy extending it, now the cubs had arrived. It had felt strange at first, and hunting for food was hard work, but they'd met a friendly fieldmouse called Capper who'd helped them to find their way around. And now they were quite used to living in the Wild.

'So – you don't regret it, then, George?' Elsie said, a little wistfully. George shook his head.

'It's different,' he said. 'Very different. But – good – you know? There's so much to see and hear and smell, and you have to be really alert. It – well – it makes you feel more alive.'

George certainly looked more alive. He looked untidy – a bit shaggy – but rugged and bold, and more mature somehow. It was as though the George she had known was just a pale imitation of this more vital, happy hamster. The cubs too were a bit unkempt, but so bright-eyed and tough-looking, Elsie couldn't get over it. And they all spoke with the accent of the Wild.

'Daisy – sends her love,' George said hesitantly. Then he said, 'You could still come with us, you know.'

For a moment a vision of this other life flashed once more into Elsie's mind. She could make her own burrow near George and the cubs and try to get on with Daisy. She could help take care of the cubs and learn to hunt for food. They would all look out for one another. But then she thought about Lucy, and as suddenly as the vision came it faded.

'No, George,' she said. 'It's not my kind of life. I – I can see that it is for you – but it's not for me.'

It was an important moment. George understood that she had come to her decision. He didn't try to talk her out of it, he just nodded, and they looked at one another quietly for a moment.

Then Elsie told him all about what had happened since he left, about making her way home with Mabel, and about Uncle Vince being caught.

'Serves him right,' said George.

He would have said more, but at that moment Danny and Donal, who had been scrapping on the top of the cage, fell right off it and George had to catch them before they rolled off the shelf and dust them down. Disturbed by the noise, Lucy moved restlessly in bed.

'We'd better go,' George said, and Elsie nodded wordlessly. 'But we'll come back,' he added, 'won't we, kiddies? What do you say to your Aunty Elsie?'

'Thank you, Aunty Elsie,' the cubs chorused, and they looked so funny, covered in food and wood-shavings, that Elsie didn't know whether to laugh or cry.

'Come and give me a hug,' she said to them. She kissed and hugged them all, though some of the boy cubs squirmed. Lastly she came to George. She hugged him, and groomed him behind his ears just as she used to, then they touched noses briefly and Elsie combed his whiskers.

It was time to go. George made many promises to visit again, soon. Elsie watched with a queer, tearing feeling in her heart as they climbed back down the canvas curtain, and one by one squeezed through the door. George and little Elsie were the last to leave and they looked back at her and waved before passing through.

'Goodbye, George dear,' Elsie called. 'Do take care! Watch out for the foxes. And the cats!'

Then they were gone, and Elsie wiped her eyes once more. But in fact she felt happier than she had in weeks, and hungry too. She scurried around her cage looking for left-over food (there wasn't much), then ran round her wheel for exercise, thinking how surprised Lucy would be in the morning, when she saw that all the food had gone.

In the next few days she kept herself busy, and started grooming herself again. She was soon the sleek tidy little hamster she had always been because she could look forward to the next visit from George, and to the day when she herself might, she just might, feel brave enough to visit him.

So the only person who wasn't very happy now was Guy. He was particularly unhappy when Matchless Mick turned up carrying a bunch of flowers for Jackie in his enormous, tattooed paw. Guy's shoulders drooped and he sat down and didn't seem to have the heart even to play his guitar. Frank didn't notice too much at first. He was busy with his own thoughts. Like:

Where was the Black Hamster now, and when would Frank see him next?

What did he mean by 'Help my people'?

Could it be that Frank was supposed to lead all

hamsters out of captivity, back to the desert city of Narkiz?

But how could he, if Narkiz was lost?

He was disturbed in these important thoughts by Guy lifting him out of his cage and sitting down with him on the settee. He let Frank run all over his shirt, which had a rough woollen texture that Frank liked to pluck, and have a good tug at the buttons. Usually it made Guy laugh when Frank explored his shirt like this, but now he kept sighing, and Frank had to dodge the smelly blasts of cheese-and-chutney flavoured breath. Eventually he stood up on Guy's chest.

'All right,' he said. 'What's the matter?'

'It's all right for you, Frank,' Guy said. 'I wish I was a hamster. No problems, no worries, nothing to do ...'

Frank was speechless.

Guy rambled on for a while about Jackie and Mick, while Frank explored his pockets. There were always some interesting things in Guy's pockets – old tickets and receipts, a wad of chewing-gum in silver paper, some rather hairy chocolate buttons and a plectrum. Guy sighed gustily again as Frank emerged, and Frank ducked.

'Why don't you play your guitar,' he said into Guy's mind. This was something he never thought he'd say, but Guy barely moved.

'There's no point even playing the guitar,' Guy said. 'No point doing anything. I'm all washed up. I'm nowhere. I haven't even got a job. Jackie was right about me ...' He trailed off into another big sigh.

It was clear to Frank that he had to do something.

He had abused his power over Guy, and now he had to do something to put it right. He looked at Guy consideringly.

'You need a job,' he thought. Frank didn't know much about human jobs, but he had heard of one ...

... Which is how Guy came to help children across the road from the school, wearing a white coat and carrying a large, lollipop-shaped sign. He seemed a bit bemused to be there, but on the whole, he discovered, he didn't mind. It got him talking, to the children and to some of the parents. One of the parents said that he played in a band in a local pub, and Guy was welcome to come along and jam with them. And Jackie thought it was wonderful, and of course, it still left him plenty of time to watch telly with Frank.

So Guy cheered up. Frank, watching him, felt that he'd done the right thing and used his power well. He began to realize that there were a lot of different ways of using it, but to use it properly meant that it worked better, and was stronger somehow. He still didn't know how he was supposed to use it to help hamsters. The thought that he might use it to lead them all from captivity was an exciting one, but he couldn't help remembering that not every hamster wanted to be released. And he didn't know where Syria was, but he had a feeling it was a lot further away than the other end of Bright Street.

Frank spent a lot of time pondering these things as he recovered his strength. He thought about Leila too, and the memory he'd shared with Chestnut. Where was she now, he wondered, and did she remember

Frank at all? Most of all he thought about the Black Hamster, and about when he would see him again. He wondered about where he was when he wasn't with Frank. How was it that he felt so real, more real than anything Frank had ever known, with a real pelt, and whiskers and blood, yet he could change size, and disappear?

No matter how hard Frank thought, he couldn't come up with any answers. Still, he felt sure that he would see the Black Hamster again, and when that time came he would make him answer some questions. In the meantime he had to be prepared – eat well, do his exercises, and try not to think too much about when that time would be. Living the life you had to live was another kind of courage after all. Not the kind you needed an exclamation mark for, like this:

Courage!

More the quiet kind, like this:

Courage.